PENGUIN POPULAR CLASSICS

THE MERCHANT OF VENICE
BY WILLIAM SHAKESPEARE

PENGUIN POPULAR CLASSICS

THE MERCHANT
OF VENICE

WILLIAM
SHAKESPEARE

PENGUIN BOOKS

PENGUIN BOOKS

Published by the Penguin Group
Penguin Books Ltd, 80 Strand, London WC2R ORL, England
Penguin Putnam Inc., 375 Hudson Street, New York, New York 10014, USA
Penguin Books Australia Ltd, Ringwood, Victoria, Australia
Penguin Books Canada Ltd, 10 Alcorn Avenue, Toronto, Ontario, Canada M4V 3B2
Penguin Books India (P) Ltd, 11 Community Centre, Panchsheel Park,
New Delhi – 110 017, India
Penguin Books (NZ) Ltd, Cnr Rosedale and Airborne Roads, Albany, Auckland,
New Zealand
Penguin Books (South Africa) (Pty) Ltd, 24 Sturdee Avenue, Rosebank 2196, South Africa

Penguin Books Ltd, Registered Offices: 80 Strand, London WC2R ORL, England

www.penguin.com

Published in Penguin Popular Classics 1994
Reprinted with line numbers 2001
13

Printed in England by Cox & Wyman Ltd, Reading, Berkshire

CONTENTS

THE WORKS OF SHAKESPEARE

PLAYS

APPROXIMATE DATE		FIRST PRINTED
Before 1594	HENRY VI *three parts*	Folio 1623
	RICHARD III	1597
	TITUS ANDRONICUS	1594
	LOVE'S LABOUR'S LOST	1598
	THE TWO GENTLEMEN OF VERONA	Folio
	THE COMEDY OF ERRORS	Folio
	THE TAMING OF THE SHREW	Folio
1594–1597	ROMEO AND JULIET (*pirated* 1597)	1599
	A MIDSUMMER NIGHT'S DREAM	1600
	RICHARD II	1597
	KING JOHN	Folio
	THE MERCHANT OF VENICE	1600
1597–1600	HENRY IV *part i*	1598
	HENRY IV *part ii*	1600
	HENRY V (*pirated* 1600)	Folio
	MUCH ADO ABOUT NOTHING	1600
	MERRY WIVES OF WINDSOR (*pirated* 1602)	Folio
	AS YOU LIKE IT	Folio
	JULIUS CAESAR	Folio
	TROYLUS AND CRESSIDA	1609
1601–1608	HAMLET (*pirated* 1603)	1604
	TWELFTH NIGHT	Folio
	MEASURE FOR MEASURE	Folio
	ALL'S WELL THAT ENDS WELL	Folio
	OTHELLO	1622
	LEAR	1608
	MACBETH	Folio
	TIMON OF ATHENS	Folio
	ANTONY AND CLEOPATRA	Folio
	CORIOLANUS	Folio
After 1608	PERICLES (*omitted from the Folio*)	1609
	CYMBELINE	Folio
	THE WINTER'S TALE	Folio
	THE TEMPEST	Folio
	HENRY VIII	Folio

POEMS

DATES UNKNOWN		
	VENUS AND ADONIS	1593
	THE RAPE OF LUCRECE	1594
	SONNETS A LOVER'S COMPLAINT }	1609
	THE PHOENIX AND THE TURTLE	1601

WILLIAM SHAKESPEARE

William Shakespeare was born at Stratford upon Avon in April, 1564. He was the third child, and eldest son, of John Shakespeare and Mary Arden. His father was one of the most prosperous men of Stratford, who held in turn the chief offices in the town. His mother was of gentle birth, the daughter of Robert Arden of Wilmcote. In December, 1582, Shakespeare married Ann Hathaway, daughter of a farmer of Shottery, near Stratford; their first child Susanna was baptized on May 6, 1583, and twins, Hamnet and Judith, on February 22, 1585. Little is known of Shakespeare's early life; but it is unlikely that a writer who dramatized such an incomparable range and variety of human kinds and experiences should have spent his early manhood entirely in placid pursuits in a country town. There is one tradition, not universally accepted, that he fled from Stratford because he was in trouble for deer stealing, and had fallen foul of Sir Thomas Lucy, the local magnate; another that he was for some time a schoolmaster.

From 1592 onwards the records are much fuller. In March, 1592, the Lord Strange's players produced a new play at the Rose Theatre called *Harry the Sixth*, which was very successful, and was probably the *First Part of Henry VI*. In the autumn of 1592 Robert Greene, the best known of the professional writers, as he was dying wrote a letter to three fellow writers in which he warned them against the ingratitude of players in general, and in particular against an 'upstart crow' who 'supposes he is as much able to bombast out a blank verse as the best of you: and being an absolute Johannes Factotum is in his own conceit the only

Shake-scene in a country'. This is the first reference to Shakespeare, and the whole passage suggests that Shakespeare had become suddenly famous as a playwright. At this time Shakespeare was brought into touch with Edward Alleyne the great tragedian, and Christopher Marlowe, whose thundering parts of Tamburlaine, the Jew of Malta, and Dr Faustus Alleyne was acting, as well as Hieronimo, the hero of Kyd's *Spanish Tragedy*, the most famous of all Elizabethan plays.

In April, 1593, Shakespeare published his poem *Venus and Adonis*, which was dedicated to the young Earl of Southampton: it was a great and lasting success, and was reprinted nine times in the next few years. In May, 1594, his second poem, *The Rape of Lucrece*, was also dedicated to Southampton.

There was little playing in 1593, for the theatres were shut during a severe outbreak of the plague; but in the autumn of 1594, when the plague ceased, the playing companies were reorganized, and Shakespeare became a sharer in the Lord Chamberlain's company who went to play in the Theatre in Shoreditch. During these months Marlowe and Kyd had died. Shakespeare was thus for a time without a rival. He had already written the three parts of *Henry VI*, *Richard III*, *Titus Andronicus*, *The Two Gentlemen of Verona*, *Love's Labour's Lost*, *The Comedy of Errors*, and *The Taming of the Shrew*. Soon afterwards he wrote the first of his greater plays – *Romeo and Juliet* – and he followed this success in the next three years with *A Midsummer Night's Dream*, *Richard II*, and *The Merchant of Venice*. The two parts of *Henry IV*, introducing Falstaff, the most popular of all his comic characters, were written in 1597–8.

The company left the Theatre in 1597 owing to disputes over a renewal of the ground lease, and went to play at the

Curtain in the same neighbourhood. The disputes continued throughout 1598, and at Christmas the players settled the matter by demolishing the old Theatre and re-erecting a new playhouse on the South bank of the Thames, near Southwark Cathedral. This playhouse was named the Globe. The expenses of the new building were shared by the chief members of the Company, including Shakespeare, who was by now a man of some means. In 1596 he had bought New Place, a large house in the centre of Stratford, for £60, and through his father purchased a coat-of-arms from the Heralds, which was the official recognition that he and his family were gentlefolk.

By the summer of 1598 Shakespeare was recognized as the greatest of English dramatists. Booksellers were printing his more popular plays, at times even in pirated or stolen versions, and he received a remarkable tribute from a young writer named Francis Meres, in his book *Palladis Tamia*. In a long catalogue of English authors Meres gave Shakespeare more prominence than any other writer, and mentioned by name twelve of his plays.

Shortly before the Globe was opened, Shakespeare had completed the cycle of plays dealing with the whole story of the Wars of the Roses with *Henry V*. It was followed by *As You Like it*, and *Julius Caesar*, the first of the maturer tragedies. In the next three years he wrote *Troylus and Cressida*, *The Merry Wives of Windsor*, *Hamlet*, and *Twelfth Night*.

On March 24, 1603, Queen Elizabeth died. The company had often performed before her, but they found her successor a far more enthusiastic patron. One of the first acts of King James was to take over the company and to promote them to be his own servants so that henceforward they were known as the King's Men. They acted now very frequently at Court, and prospered accordingly. In the early years of the reign Shakespeare wrote the more sombre comedies, *All's Well that Ends Well*, and *Measure for Measure*, which were followed by *Othello*, *Macbeth*, and *King Lear*. Then he returned to Roman themes with *Antony and Cleopatra* and *Coriolanus*.

Since 1601 Shakespeare had been writing less, and there were now a number of rival dramatists who were introducing new styles of drama, particularly Ben Jonson (whose first successful comedy, *Every Man in his Humour*, was acted by Shakespeare's company in 1598), Chapman, Dekker, Marston, and Beaumont and Fletcher who began to write in 1607. In 1608 the King's Men acquired a second playhouse, an indoor private theatre in the fashionable quarter of the Blackfriars. At private theatres, plays were performed indoors; the prices charged were higher than in the public playhouses, and the audience consequently was more select. Shakespeare seems to have retired from the stage about this time: his name does not occur in the various lists of players after 1607. Henceforward he lived for the most part at Stratford, where he was regarded as one of the most important citizens. He still wrote a few plays, and he tried his hand at the new form of tragi-comedy – a play with tragic incidents but a happy ending – which Beaumont and Fletcher had popularized. He wrote four of these – *Pericles, Cymbeline, The Winter's Tale*, and *The Tempest*, which was acted at Court in 1611. For the last four years of his life he lived in retirement. His son Hamnet had died in 1596: his two daughters were now married. Shakespeare died at Stratford upon Avon on April 23, 1616, and was buried in the chancel of the church, before the high altar. Shortly afterwards a memorial which still exists, with a portrait bust, was set up on the North wall. His wife survived him.

When Shakespeare died fourteen of his plays had been separately published in Quarto booklets. In 1623 his surviving fellow actors, John Heming and Henry Condell, with the co-operation of a number of printers, published a collected edition of thirty-six plays in one Folio volume, with an engraved portrait, memorial verses by Ben Jonson and others, and an Epistle to the Reader in which Heming and Condell make the interesting note that Shakespeare's 'hand and mind went together, and what he thought, he uttered with that easiness that we have scarce received from him a blot in his papers.'

The plays as printed in the Quartos or the Folio differ considerably from the usual modern text. They are often not divided into scenes, and sometimes not even into acts. Nor are there place-headings at the beginning of each scene, because in the Elizabethan theatre there was no scenery. They are carelessly printed and the spelling is erratic.

THE ELIZABETHAN THEATRE

Although plays of one sort and another had been acted for many generations, no permanent playhouse was erected in England until 1576. In the 1570's the Lord Mayor and Aldermen of the City of London and the players were constantly at variance. As a result James Burbage, then the leader of the great Earl of Leicester's players, decided that he would erect a playhouse outside the jurisdiction of the Lord Mayor, where the players would no longer be hindered by the authorities. Accordingly in 1576 he built the Theatre in Shoreditch, at that time a suburb of London. The experiment was successful, and by 1592 there were two more playhouses in London, the Curtain (also in Shore-ditch), and the Rose on the south bank of the river, near Southwark Cathedral.

Elizabethan players were accustomed to act on a variety of stages; in the great hall of a nobleman's house, or one of the Queen's palaces, in town halls and in yards, as well as their own theatre.

The public playhouse for which most of Shakespeare's plays were written was a small and intimate affair. The outside measurement of the Fortune Theatre, which was built in 1600 to rival the new Globe, was but eighty feet square. Playhouses were usually circular or octagonal, with three tiers of galleries looking down upon the yard or pit, which was open to the sky. The stage jutted out into the yard so that the actors came forward into the midst of their audience.

Over the stage there was a roof, and on either side doors by which the characters entered or disappeared. Over the back of the stage ran a gallery or upper stage which was used whenever an upper scene was needed, as when Romeo climbs up to Juliet's bedroom, or the citizens of Angiers address King John from the walls. The space beneath this upper stage was known as the tiring house; it was concealed from the audience by a curtain which would be drawn back to reveal an inner stage, for such scenes as the witches' cave in Macbeth, Prospero's cell or Juliet's tomb.

There was no general curtain concealing the whole stage, so that all scenes on the main stage began with an entrance and ended with an exit. Thus in tragedies the dead must be carried away. There was no scenery, and therefore no limit to the number of scenes, for a scene came to an end when the characters left the stage. When it was necessary for the exact locality of a scene to be known, then Shakespeare

THE GLOBE THEATRE
Wood-engraving by R. J. Beedham after a reconstruction by J. C. Adams

indicated it in the dialogue; otherwise a simple property or a garment was sufficient; a chair or stool showed an indoor scene, a man wearing riding boots was a messenger, a king wearing armour was on the battlefield, or the like. Such simplicity was on the whole an advantage; the spectator was not distracted by the setting and Shakespeare was able to use as many scenes as he wished. The action passed by very quickly: a play of 2500 lines of verse could be acted in two hours. Moreover, since the actor was so close to his audience, the slightest subtlety of voice and gesture was easily appreciated.

The company was a 'Fellowship of Players', who were all partners and sharers. There were usually ten to fifteen full members, with three or four boys, and some paid servants. Shakespeare had therefore to write for his team. The chief actor in the company was Richard Burbage, who first distinguished himself as Richard III; for him Shakespeare wrote his great tragic parts. An important member of the company was the clown or low comedian. From 1594 to 1600 the company's clown was Will Kemp; he was succeeded by Robert Armin. No women were allowed to appear on the stage, and all women's parts were taken by boys.

*

THE MERCHANT OF VENICE

The Merchant of Venice was written some time before 1598, and probably in 1596. It is mentioned amongst the twelve plays in Meres' list in *Palladis Tamia* (see page 9). It was acted at Whitehall on 10 February 1605, before King James the First, who was so pleased that he ordered it to be played again on the following Tuesday.

The story of the Jew and the Merchant seems to have been dramatized long before Shakespeare's time. In 1579, for instance, Stephen Gosson in his *School of Abuse* mentioned a play of the Jew shown at the Bull 'representing the greediness of worldly choosers, and bloody minds of usurers'. If this is an early version of *The Merchant of Venice*, then it derived from a story in Ser Giovanni's *Il Pecorone*, written in the fourteenth century, and printed in 1558. In this tale Giannetto of Venice sought the hand of the Lady of Belmonte. The condition laid on every suitor was that he should remain awake all night, otherwise he lost his ship and cargo. Giannetto failed twice; but the third time he was successful. For these ventures he borrowed money from Ansaldo his godfather, who financed the first two himself, but for the third was obliged to borrow 10,000 ducats from a Jew, on condition that if he failed to repay the money by Saint John's Day the Jew should cut off a pound of his flesh. Giannetto, having successfully married the Lady of Belmonte, forgot about his godfather until, being by chance reminded that it was Saint John's Day, he realized his godfather's danger, and set off for Venice to rescue him or to bid him farewell. In Venice he found that the Jew was demanding the fulfilment of his contract, but had granted

Ansaldo a few days' respite in case Giannetto should return. Giannetto offered up to 100,000 ducats to cancel the bond; but all his proposals were refused. While the argument was going on the Lady of Belmonte herself arrived in Venice disguised as a Doctor of Laws, and lodged at the same inn as her husband. The supposed Doctor then gave out that he was prepared to settle any dispute on a matter of law, and Giannetto appeared before him with the Jew, whom the Doctor outwitted in the same manner as Portia defeats Shylock. The matter being satisfactorily settled, the Doctor refused to accept any money, but asked for the ring on Giannetto's hand, which Giannetto was very reluctant to give, but at last yielded. After merrymaking in Venice, Giannetto then returned with his godfather Ansaldo and his friends to Belmonte. As soon as he arrived his wife demanded where the ring was and accused him of giving it to one of his old sweethearts in Venice. This Giannetto denied indignantly and burst into tears. Whereupon the Lady of Belmonte, perceiving the joke had gone far enough, showed the ring and explained everything.

Similar stories of the tricking of an unjust creditor are not uncommon in medieval and oriental Tales. So, too, are various versions of the Choosing of the Caskets. Shakespeare was thus dramatizing fairy tales which in some form or other were very old and widely known.

In creating the character of Shylock Shakespeare borrowed something from Marlowe's *Jew of Malta*. Marlowe wrote the play about 1590; it had been a great success, and was still being played. Barabbas, Marlowe's Jew, like Shylock, had an only daughter and many ducats. He had a hatred of all Christians, as was not unreasonable for Italian Jews, but he is a more ferocious (and far less credible) figure than Shylock, with the power and the will to achieve orgies of vengeance. Barabbas lived mainly to revenge his race, and his soliloquies expressed a vindictive and relentless nature which was regarded as typical of the Jews in Shakespeare's time:

> I am not of the tribe of Levi, I,
> That can so soon forget an injury.
> We Jews can fawn like spaniels when we please;
> And when we grin we bite; yet are our looks
> As innocent and harmless as a lamb's.
> I learn'd in Florence how to kiss my hand,
> Heave up my shoulders when they call me dog,
> And duck as low as any bare-foot friar;
> Hoping to see them starve upon a stall,
> Or else be gather'd for in our synagogue,
> That, when the offering-basin comes to me,
> Even for charity I may spit into't.

This anti-Jewish feeling had been considerably increased since Marlowe's play was first produced, after the sensational case of Dr Roderigo Lopez. Lopez was a Portuguese Jew who had fled to England in 1559 and set up as a doctor. In time his practice had grown, and he had been appointed Physician to the Queen. Lopez had many underhand dealings with the spies who peddled information between England and Spain, but fell foul of the Earl of Essex. Early in 1594 Essex believed that he had found good evidence for supposing that Lopez was accepting bribes from the Spanish King to poison Queen Elizabeth. Lopez was arrested, and broke down under cross-examination. It is very doubtful whether he ever intended any harm against the Queen, but he may have been ready to poison Don Antonio, the ex-King of Portugal, who was living in England. He was tried with other accomplices at the Guildhall, and found guilty.

The Queen at first refused to believe in his guilt, but he was eventually executed on the 7th June. On the scaffold Lopez protested his innocence, declaring that 'he loved the Queen as well as he loved Jesus Christ, which, coming from a man of the Jewish profession, moved no small laughter in the standers-by'. Whatever the truth of the case, it confirmed the general prejudice that Jews would stop at nothing when dealing with Christians.

Shakespeare also borrowed something from his own play *The Two Gentlemen of Verona*. The scene where Portia and Nerissa discuss the various suitors (p. 29) had already appeared in *The Two Gentlemen* where Julia runs over the points of her wooers with Lucetta (Act I, Scene 2); and Lancelot Gobbo is a re-incarnation of Launce.

The Merchant of Venice was entered in the Stationers' Register on 22 July 1598 – 'to James Roberts, provided that it be not printed by the said James Roberts or any other whatsoever, without licence first had from the Right Honourable the Lord Chamberlain'. The probable purpose of this entry was to prevent publication. From time to time Roberts entered plays of the Chamberlain's Men to secure the copyright, but without any intention of printing them. On 28 October 1600, by consent of Roberts the play was again entered by Thomas Heyes who brought out an edition soon afterwards. This Quarto is entitled '*The most excellent Historie of the Merchant of Venice. With the extreame crueltie of Shylocke the Iewe towards the sayd Merchant, in cutting a iust pound of his flesh : and the obtayning of Portia by the choyse of three chests. As it hath beene diuers times acted by the Lord Chamberlaine his Seruants. Written by William Shakespeare. AT LONDON, Printed by I. R. for Thomas Heyes, and are to be sold in Paules Church-yard, at the signe of the Greene Dragon. 1600*'.

This text is, on the whole, well printed, except for certain peculiarities. The printer was apparently short of capital letters, especially of capital I's. The result is that many of the verse lines begin with small letters, and a large number of capital I's are in italic type. He was also short of full stops, but well supplied with question marks, which he used instead. This Quarto was reprinted in 1619 by Jaggard, the printer, with others of Shakespeare's plays. As, however, Jaggard did not possess the copyright, he added on the title page the words 'Printed by J. Roberts, 1600'. Jaggard's Quarto was for long regarded as the original first edition, and modern editions were until recently based on it.

In the First Folio of 1623 the text was set up from a copy of Heyes' Quarto which it follows very closely. It has been lightly corrected; the missing capital letters have been replaced, but the abundant question marks remain, and there are some new misprints. This copy of the Quarto had apparently been used in the playhouse, for it adds a few stage directions, chiefly concerned with the music.

There is little to choose between the Quarto and Folio; but as the Folio text was a playhouse copy it seemed more desirable to use it for this edition. It has been followed closely, and its few errors corrected by the Quarto.

Spelling is modernized, but the original arrangement, and the punctuation (which according to Elizabethan practice 'points' the text for reading aloud) have been kept, except where they seemed obviously wrong. The reader who is used to an 'accepted text' may thus find certain unfamiliarities, but the present text is nearer to that used in Shakespeare's own playhouse.

The Merchant of
Venice

THE ACTORS' NAMES

The DUKE OF VENICE
The PRINCE OF MOROCCO, }
The PRINCE OF ARRAGON, } suitors to Portia
ANTONIO, a Merchant of Venice
BASSANIO, his friend, suitor likewise to Portia
SOLANIO, }
SALARINO, } friends to Antonio and Bassanio
GRATIANO, }
LORENZO, in love with Jessica
SALERIO, a messenger from Venice
SHYLOCK, a rich Jew
TUBAL, a Jew, his friend
LAUNCELOT GOBBO, the Clown, servant to Shylock
OLD GOBBO, father to Launcelot
LEONARDO, servant to Bassanio
BALTHASAR, }
STEPHANO, } servants to Portia
PORTIA, a rich heiress
NERISSA, her gentlewoman
JESSICA, daughter to Shylock

I. 1

Enter Antonio, Salarino, and Solanio.

ANTONIO: In sooth I know not why I am so sad,
  It wearies me: you say it wearies you;
  But how I caught it, found it, or came by it,   5
  What stuff 'tis made of, whereof it is born,
  I am to learn: and such a want-wit sadness makes of me,
  That I have much ado to know myself.

SOLANIO: Your mind is tossing on the Ocean,
  There where your Argosies with portly sail   10
  Like Signiors and rich burghers on the flood,
  Or as it were the pageants of the sea,
  Do over-peer the petty traffickers
  That curtsy to them, do them reverence
  As they fly by them with their woven wings.   15

SALARINO: Believe me sir, had I such venture forth,
  The better part of my affections, would
  Be with my hopes abroad. I should be still
  Plucking the grass to know where sits the wind,
  Peering in maps for ports, and piers, and roads: 20
  And every object that might make me fear
  Misfortune to my ventures, out of doubt
  Would make me sad.

SOLANIO: My wind cooling my broth,
  Would blow me to an ague, when I thought   25
  What harm a wind too great might do at sea.
  I should not see the sandy hour-glass run,
  But I should think of shallows, and of flats,
  And see my wealthy *Andrew* dock'd in sand,
  Vailing her high top lower than her ribs   30
  To kiss her burial; should I go to church

And see the holy edifice of stone,
And not bethink me straight of dangerous rocks,
Which touching but my gentle vessel's side
Would scatter all her spices on the stream,
5   Enrobe the roaring waters with my silks,
And in a word, but even now worth this,
And now worth nothing. Shall I have the thought
To think on this, and shall I lack the thought
That such a thing bechanc'd would make me sad?
10   But tell not me, I know Antonio
Is sad to think upon his merchandise.

ANTONIO: Believe me no, I thank my fortune for it,
My ventures are not in one bottom trusted,
Nor to one place; nor is my whole estate
15   Upon the fortune of this present year:
Therefore my merchandise makes me not sad.

SOLANIO: Why then you are in love.

ANTONIO: Fie, fie.

SOLANIO: Not in love neither: then let us say you are sad
20   Because you are not merry; and 'twere as easy
For you to laugh and leap, and say you are merry
Because you are not sad. Now by two-headed Janus,
Nature hath fram'd strange fellows in her time:
Some that will evermore peep through their eyes,
25   And laugh like parrots at a bag-piper.
And other of such vinegar aspect,
That they'll not show their teeth in way of smile,
Though Nestor swear the jest be laughable.
        Enter Bassanio, Lorenzo, and Gratiano.
30 SOLANIO: Here comes Bassanio, your most noble kinsman,
Gratiano, and Lorenzo. Fare ye well,
We leave you now with better company.

SALARINO: I would have stay'd till I had made you merry,

If worthier friends had not prevented me.

ANTONIO: Your worth is very dear in my regard.
  I take it your own business calls on you,
  And you embrace th' occasion to depart.

SOLANIO: Good morrow my good Lords.   5

BASSANIO: Good signiors both, when shall we laugh? say,
    when?
  You grow exceeding strange: must it be so?

SOLANIO: We'll make our leisures to attend on yours.
              Exeunt Salarino and Solanio.   10

LORENZO: My Lord Bassanio, since you have found
    Antonio
  We two will leave you, but at dinner-time
  I pray you have in mind where we must meet.

BASSANIO: I will not fail you.   15

GRATIANO: You look not well Signior Antonio,
  You have too much respect upon the world:
  They lose it that do buy it with much care,
  Believe me you are marvellously chang'd.

ANTONIO: I hold the world but as the world Gratiano,   20
  A stage, where every man must play a part,
  And mine a sad one.

GRATIANO: Let me play the fool,
  With mirth and laughter let old wrinkles come,
  And let my liver rather heat with wine,   25
  Than my heart cool with mortifying groans.
  Why should a man whose blood is warm within,
  Sit like his grandsire, cut in alablaster?
  Sleep when he wakes? and creep into the jaundice
  By being peevish? I tell thee what Antonio,   30
  I love thee, and it is my love that speaks:
  There are a sort of men, whose visages
  Do cream and mantle like a standing pond,

And do a wilful stillness entertain,
With purpose to be dress'd in an opinion
Of wisdom, gravity, profound conceit,
As who should say, I am Sir Oracle,
5   And when I ope my lips, let no dog bark.
O my Antonio, I do know of these
That therefore only are reputed wise,
For saying nothing; when I am very sure
If they should speak, would almost dam those ears
10 Which hearing them would call their brothers fools:
I'll tell thee more of this another time.
But fish not with this melancholy bait
For this fool gudgeon, this opinion:
Come good Lorenzo, fare ye well awhile,
15 I'll end my exhortation after dinner.

LORENZO: Well, we will leave you then till dinner time.
I must be one of these same dumb wise men,
For Gratiano never lets me speak.

GRATIANO: Well, keep me company but two years mo,
20 Thou shalt not know the sound of thine own tongue.

ANTONIO: Fare you well, I'll grow a talker for this gear.

GRATIANO: Thanks i' faith, for silence is only commendable
In a neat's tongue dried, and a maid not vendible.

25   *Exeunt Gratiano and Lorenzo.*

ANTONIO: Is that any thing now?

BASSANIO: Gratiano speaks an infinite deal of nothing,
more than any man in all Venice, his reasons are as two
grains of wheat hid in two bushels of chaff: you shall seek
30 all day ere you find them, and when you have them they
are not worth the search.

ANTONIO: Well: tell me now, what Lady is the same
To whom you swore a secret pilgrimage

That you today promis'd to tell me of?
BASSANIO: 'Tis not unknown to you Antonio
How much I have disabled mine estate,
By something showing a more swelling port
Than my faint means would grant continuance: 5
Nor do I now make moan to be abridg'd
From such a noble rate, but my chief care
Is to come fairly off from the great debts
Wherein my time something too prodigal
Hath left me gag'd: to you Antonio   10
I owe the most in money, and in love,
And from your love I have a warranty
To unburthen all my plots and purposes,
How to get clear of all the debts I owe.
ANTONIO: I pray you good Bassanio let me know it,   15
And if it stand as you yourself still do,
Within the eye of honour, be assur'd
My purse, my person, my extremest means
Lie all unlock'd to your occasions.
BASSANIO: In my school days, when I had lost one shaft   20
I shot his fellow of the selfsame flight
The selfsame way, with more advised watch
To find the other forth, and by adventuring both,
I oft found both. I urge this childhood proof,
Because what follows is pure innocence.   25
I owe you much, and like a wilful youth,
That which I owe is lost: but if you please
To shoot another arrow that self way
Which you did shoot the first, I do not doubt,
As I will watch the aim, or to find both,   30
Or bring your latter hazard back again,
And thankfully rest debtor for the first.
ANTONIO: You know me well, and herein spend but time

To wind about my love with circumstance,
And out of doubt you do me now more wrong
In making question of my uttermost
Than if you had made waste of all I have:
5   Then do but say to me what I should do
That in your knowledge may by me be done,
And I am prest unto it: therefore speak.
  BASSANIO: In Belmont is a Lady richly left,
And she is fair, and fairer than that word,
10   Of wondrous virtues, sometimes from her eyes
I did receive fair speechless messages:
Her name is Portia, nothing undervalu'd
To Cato's daughter, Brutus' Portia,
Nor is the wide world ignorant of her worth,
15   For the four winds blow in from every coast
Renowned suitors, and her sunny locks
Hang on her temples like a golden fleece,
Which makes her seat of Belmont Colchos' strond,
And many Jasons come in quest of her.
20   O my Antonio, had I but the means
To hold a rival place with one of them,
I have a mind presages me such thrift,
That I should questionless be fortunate.
  ANTONIO: Thou know'st that all my fortunes are at sea,
25   Neither have I money, nor commodity
To raise a present sum, therefore go forth
Try what my credit can in Venice do,
That shall be rack'd even to the uttermost,
To furnish thee to Belmont to fair Portia.
30   Go presently inquire, and so will I
Where money is, and I no question make
To have it of my trust, or for my sake.

                        Exeunt.

I.2

Enter Portia with her waiting woman Nerissa.

PORTIA: By my troth Nerissa, my little body is aweary of
this great world.

NERISSA: You would be sweet Madam, if your miseries   5
were in the same abundance as your good fortunes are:
and yet for aught I see, they are as sick that surfeit with
too much, as they that starve with nothing; it is no small
happiness therefore to be seated in the mean, superfluity
comes sooner by white hairs, but competency lives   10
longer.

PORTIA: Good sentences, and well pronounc'd.

NERISSA: They would be better if well followed.

PORTIA: If to do were as easy as to know what were good
to do, chapels had been churches, and poor men's cot-   15
tages Princes' palaces: it is a good divine that follows his
own instructions; I can easier teach twenty what were
good to be done, than be one of the twenty to follow
mine own teaching: the brain may devise laws for the
blood, but a hot temper leaps o'er a cold decree, such a   20
hare is madness the youth, to skip o'er the meshes of good
counsel the cripple; but this reasoning is not in the fashion
to choose me a husband: O me, the word choose, I may
neither choose whom I would, nor refuse whom I dislike,
so is the will of a living daughter curb'd by the will of a   25
dead father: is it not hard Nerissa, that I cannot choose
one, nor refuse none?

NERISSA: Your father was ever virtuous, and holy men at
their death have good inspirations, therefore the lottery
that he hath devised in these three chests of gold, silver,   30
and lead, whereof who chooses his meaning, chooses you,

will no doubt never be chosen by any rightly, but one who you shall rightly love: but what warmth is there in your affection towards any of these princely suitors that are already come?

5 PORTIA: I pray thee over-name them, and as thou namest them, I will describe them, and according to my description level at my affection.

NERISSA: First there is the Neapolitan Prince.

PORTIA: Ay that's a colt indeed, for he doth nothing but
10 talk of his horse, and he makes it a great appropriation to his own good parts that he can shoe him himself: I am much afraid my Lady his mother played false with a smith.

NERISSA: Then is there the County Palentine.

PORTIA: He doth nothing but frown (as who should say,
15 and you will not have me, choose: he hears merry tales and smiles not, I fear he will prove the weeping philosopher when he grows old, being so full of unmannerly sadness in his youth). I had rather be married to a death's head with a bone in his mouth, than to either of these:
20 God defend me from these two.

NERISSA: How say you by the French Lord, Mounsier Le Boune?

PORTIA: God made him, and therefore let him pass for a man; in truth I know it is a sin to be a mocker, but he,
25 why he hath a horse better than the Neapolitan's, a better bad habit of frowning than the Count Palentine, he is every man in no man, if a trassell sing, he falls straight a capering, he will fence with his own shadow. If I should marry him, I should marry twenty husbands: if he would
30 despise me, I would forgive him, for if he love me to madness, I should never requite him.

NERISSA: What say you then to Fauconbridge, the young Baron of England?

PORTIA: You know I say nothing to him, for he understands not me, nor I him: he hath neither Latin, French,
nor Italian, and you will come into the Court and swear
that I have a poor pennyworth in the English: he is a
proper man's picture, but alas who can converse with a 5
dumb show? how oddly he is suited, I think he bought his
doublet in Italy, his round hose in France, his bonnet in
Germany, and his behaviour every where.

NERISSA: What think you of the Scottish Lord his neighbour? 10

PORTIA: That he hath a neighbourly charity in him, for he
borrowed a box of the ear of the Englishman, and swore
he would pay him again when he was able: I think the
Frenchman became his surety, and seal'd under for another. 15

NERISSA: How like you the young German, the Duke of
Saxony's nephew?

PORTIA: Very vilely in the morning when he is sober, and
most vilely in the afternoon when he is drunk: when he
is best, he is a little worse than a man, and when he is 20
worst he is little better than a beast: and the worst fall
that ever fell, I hope I shall make shift to go without him.

NERISSA: If he should offer to choose, and choose the right
casket, you should refuse to perform your Father's will,
if you should refuse to accept him. 25

PORTIA: Therefore for fear of the worst, I pray thee set a
deep glass of Rhenish wine on the contrary casket, for if
the devil be within, and that temptation without, I know
he will choose it. I will do any thing Nerissa ere I will be
married to a sponge. 30

NERISSA: You need not fear Lady the having any of these
Lords, they have acquainted me with their determina-
tions, which is indeed to return to their home, and to

trouble you with no more suit, unless you may be won
by some other sort than your Father's imposition, de-
pending on the caskets.

PORTIA: If I live to be as old as Sibylla, I will die as chaste
5   as Diana: unless I be obtained by the manner of my
Father's will: I am glad this parcel of wooers are so rea-
sonable, for there is not one among them but I dote on
his very absence: and I pray God grant them a fair de-
parture.

10 NERISSA: Do you not remember Lady in your Father's
time, a Venetian, a scholar and a soldier that came hither
in company of the Marquis of Mountferrat?

PORTIA: Yes, yes, it was Bassanio, as I think, so was he
call'd.

15 NERISSA: True Madam, he of all the men that ever my
foolish eyes look'd upon, was the best deserving a fair
Lady.

PORTIA: I remember him well, and I remember him worthy of thy praise.

20 How now, what news?

          Enter a Servingman.

SERVINGMAN: The four strangers seek you Madam to
take their leave: and there is a fore-runner come from a
fifth, the Prince of Morocco, who brings word the
25   Prince his master will be here tonight.

PORTIA: If I could bid the fifth welcome with so good
heart as I can bid the other four farewell, I should be glad
of his approach: if he have the condition of a saint, and
the complexion of a devil, I had rather he should shrive
30   me than wive me. Come Nerissa, sirrah go before;
whiles we shut the gate upon one wooer, another knocks
at the door.

          Exeunt.

I. 3

Enter Bassanio with Shylock the Jew.

SHYLOCK: Three thousand ducats, well.

BASSANIO: Ay sir, for three months.

SHYLOCK: For three months, well.   5

BASSANIO: For the which, as I told you,
Antonio shall be bound.

SHYLOCK: Antonio shall become bound, well.

BASSANIO: May you stead me? Will you pleasure me?
Shall I know your answer?   10

SHYLOCK: Three thousand ducats for three months, and
Antonio bound.

BASSANIO: Your answer to that.

SHYLOCK: Antonio is a good man.

BASSANIO: Have you heard any imputation to the con- 15
trary?

SHYLOCK: Ho no, no, no, no: my meaning in saying he is
a good man, is to have you understand me that he is
sufficient, yet his means are in supposition: he hath an
Argosy bound to Tripolis, another to the Indies, I under- 20
stand moreover upon the Rialto, he hath a third at
Mexico, a fourth for England, and other ventures he hath
squander'd abroad, but ships are but boards, sailors but
men, there be land rats, and water rats, water thieves, and
land thieves, I mean pirates, and then there is the peril of 25
waters, winds, and rocks: the man is notwithstanding
sufficient, three thousand ducats, I think I may take his
bond.

BASSANIO: Be assured you may.

SHYLOCK: I will be assured I may: and that I may be 30
assured, I will bethink me, may I speak with Antonio?

BASSANIO: If it please you to dine with us.

SHYLOCK: Yes, to smell pork, to eat of the habitation
which your Prophet the Nazarite conjured the devil into:
I will buy with you, sell with you, talk with you, walk
5   with you, and so following: but I will not eat with you,
drink with you, nor pray with you. What news on the
Rialto, who is he comes here?

Enter Antonio.

BASSANIO: This is Signior Antonio.

10 SHYLOCK: How like a fawning publican he looks.
I hate him for he is a Christian:
But more, for that in low simplicity
He lends out money gratis, and brings down
The rate of usance here with us in Venice.
15   If I can catch him once upon the hip,
I will feed fat the ancient grudge I bear him.
He hates our sacred Nation, and he rails
Even there where merchants most do congregate
On me, my bargains, and my well-won thrift,
20   Which he calls interest: cursed be my Tribe
If I forgive him.

BASSANIO: Shylock, do you hear.

SHYLOCK: I am debating of my present store,
And by the near guess of my memory
25   I cannot instantly raise up the gross
Of full three thousand ducats: what of that?
Tubal a wealthy Hebrew of my Tribe
Will furnish me; but soft, how many months
Do you desire? Rest you fair good signior,
30   Your worship was the last man in our mouths.

ANTONIO: Shylock, albeit I neither lend nor borrow
By taking, nor by giving of excess,
Yet to supply the ripe wants of my friend,

I'll break a custom: is he yet possess'd
How much ye would?

SHYLOCK: Ay, ay, three thousand ducats.

ANTONIO: And for three months.

SHYLOCK: I had forgot, three months, you told me so.   5
Well then, your bond: and let me see, but hear you,
Methoughts you said, you neither lend nor borrow
Upon advantage.

ANTONIO: I do never use it.

SHYLOCK: When Jacob graz'd his Uncle Laban's sheep,   10
This Jacob from our holy Abram was
(As his wise mother wrought in his behalf)
The third possessor; ay, he was the third.

ANTONIO: And what of him, did he take interest?

SHYLOCK: No, not take interest, not as you would say   15
Directly interest, mark what Jacob did,
When Laban and himself were compromis'd
That all the eanlings which were streak'd and pied
Should fall as Jacob's hire, the ewes being rank,
In end of Autumn turned to the rams,   20
And when the work of generation was
Between these woolly breeders in the act,
The skilful shepherd pill'd me certain wands,
And in the doing of the deed of kind,
He stuck them up before the fulsome ewes,   25
Who then conceiving, did in eaning time
Fall parti-colour'd lambs, and those were Jacob's.
This was a way to thrive, and he was blest:
And thrift is blessing if men steal it not.

ANTONIO: This was a venture sir that Jacob serv'd for,   30
A thing not in his power to bring to pass,
But sway'd and fashion'd by the hand of heaven.
Was this inserted to make interest good?

Or is your gold and silver ewes and rams?

SHYLOCK: I cannot tell, I make it breed as fast,
But note me signior.

ANTONIO: Mark you this Bassanio,
5   The devil can cite Scripture for his purpose,
An evil soul producing holy witness,
Is like a villain with a smiling cheek,
A goodly apple rotten at the heart.
O what a goodly outside falsehood hath.

10   SHYLOCK: Three thousand ducats, 'tis a good round sum.
Three months from twelve, then let me see the rate.

ANTONIO: Well Shylock, shall we be beholding to you?

SHYLOCK: Signior Antonio, many a time and oft
In the Rialto you have rated me
15   About my moneys and my usances:
Still have I borne it with a patient shrug,
(For sufferance is the badge of all our Tribe).
You call me misbeliever, cut-throat dog,
And spet upon my Jewish gaberdine,
20   And all for use of that which is mine own.
Well then, it now appears you need my help:
Go to then, you come to me, and you say,
Shylock, we would have moneys, you say so:
You that did void your rheum upon my beard,
25   And foot me as you spurn a stranger cur
Over your threshold, moneys is your suit.
What should I say to you? Should I not say,
Hath a dog money? Is it possible
A cur can lend three thousand ducats? or
30   Shall I bend low, and in a bondman's key
With bated breath, and whisp'ring humbleness,
Say this: Fair sir, you spet on me on Wednesday last;
You spurn'd me such a day; another time

You call'd me dog: and for these courtesies
I'll lend you thus much moneys.
ANTONIO: I am as like to call thee so again,
To spet on thee again, to spurn thee too.
If thou wilt lend this money, lend it not   5
As to thy friends, for when did friendship take
A breed of barren metal of his friend?
But lend it rather to thine enemy,
Who if he break, thou mayest with better face
Exact the penalties.   10
SHYLOCK: Why look you how you storm,
I would be friends with you, and have your love,
Forget the shames that you have stain'd me with,
Supply your present wants, and take no doit
Of usance for my moneys, and you'll not hear me,   15
This is kind I offer.
BASSANIO: This were kindness.
SHYLOCK: This kindness will I show,
Go with me to a Notary, seal me there
Your single bond, and in a merry sport,   20
If you repay me not on such a day,
In such a place, such sum or sums as are
Express'd in the condition, let the forfeit
Be nominated for an equal pound
Of your fair flesh, to be cut off and taken   25
In what part of your body pleaseth me.
ANTONIO: Content in faith, I'll seal to such a bond,
And say there is much kindness in the Jew.
BASSANIO: You shall not seal to such a bond for me,
I'll rather dwell in my necessity.   30
ANTONIO: Why fear not man, I will not forfeit it,
Within these two months, that's a month before
This bond expires, I do expect return

Of thrice three times the value of this bond.

SHYLOCK: O father Abram, what these Christians are,
Whose own hard dealings teaches them suspect
The thoughts of others: Pray you tell me this,
5   If he should break his day, what should I gain
By the exaction of the forfeiture?
A pound of man's flesh taken from a man,
Is not so estimable, profitable neither
As flesh of muttons, beefs, or goats, I say
10   To buy his favour, I extend this friendship,
If he will take it, so: if not adieu,
And for my love I pray you wrong me not.

ANTONIO: Yes Shylock, I will seal unto this bond.

SHYLOCK: Then meet me forthwith at the Notary's,
15   Give him direction for this merry bond,
And I will go and purse the ducats straight.
See to my house left in the fearful guard
Of an unthrifty knave: and presently
I'll be with you.

20   *Exit Shylock.*

ANTONIO: Hie thee gentle Jew. This Hebrew will turn
Christian, he grows kind.

BASSANIO: I like not fair terms, and a villain's mind.

ANTONIO: Come on, in this there can be no dismay,
25   My ships come home a month before the day.

                    Exeunt.

II. 1

*Enter Morocco, a tawny Moor all in white, and three or
four followers accordingly, with Portia, Nerissa, and their train.*
30   *Flourish cornets.*

MOROCCO: Mislike me not for my complexion,

The shadowed livery of the burnish'd sun,
To whom I am a neighbour, and near bred.
Bring me the fairest creature northward born,
Where Phoebus' fire scarce thaws the icicles,
And let us make incision for your love,   5
To prove whose blood is reddest, his or mine.
I tell thee Lady this aspect of mine
Hath fear'd the valiant, (by my love I swear)
The best regarded virgins of our clime
Have lov'd it too: I would not change this hue,   10
Except to steal your thoughts my gentle Queen.

PORTIA: In terms of choice I am not solely led
By nice direction of a maiden's eyes:
Besides, the lottery of my destiny
Bars me the right of voluntary choosing: 15
But if my Father had not scanted me,
And hedg'd me by his wit to yield myself
His wife, who wins me by that means I told you,
Yourself (renowned Prince) then stood as fair
As any comer I have look'd on yet   20
For my affection.

MOROCCO: Even for that I thank you,
Therefore I pray you lead me to the caskets
To try my fortune: by this scimitar
That slew the Sophy, and a Persian Prince   25
That won three fields of Sultan Solyman,
I would o'er-stare the sternest eyes that look:
Out-brave the heart most daring on the earth:
Pluck the young sucking cubs from the she bear,
Yea, mock the lion when he roars for prey   30
To win the Lady. But alas, the while,
If Hercules and Lichas play at dice
Which is the better man, the greater throw

    May turn by fortune from the weaker hand:
    So is Alcides beaten by his rage,
    And so may I, blind fortune leading me
    Miss that which one unworthier may attain,
5   And die with grieving.
  PORTIA: You must take your chance,
    And either not attempt to choose at all,
    Or swear before you choose, if you choose wrong
    Never to speak to Lady afterward
10   In way of marriage, therefore be advis'd.
  MOROCCO: Nor will not, come bring me unto my chance.
  PORTIA: First forward to the temple, after dinner
    Your hazard shall be made.
  MOROCCO: Good fortune then,
15   *Cornets.*
  To make me blest or cursed'st among men.
                   Exeunt.

II. 2

Enter the Clown alone.

20 LAUNCELOT: Certainly, my conscience will serve me to
    run from this Jew my master: the fiend is at mine elbow,
    and tempts me, saying to me, Gobbo, Launcelot Gobbo,
    good Launcelot, or good Gobbo, or good Launcelot
    Gobbo, use your legs, take the start, run away: my con-
25   science says no; take heed honest Launcelot, take heed
    honest Gobbo, or as afore-said honest Launcelot Gobbo,
    do not run, scorn running with thy heels; well, the most
    courageous fiend bids me pack, *via* says the fiend, away
    says the fiend, for the heavens rouse up a brave mind says
30   the fiend, and run; well, my conscience hanging about the
    neck of my heart, says very wisely to me: My honest

friend Launcelot, being an honest man's son, or rather an
honest woman's son, for indeed my Father did something
smack, something grow to; he had a kind of taste; well,
my conscience says Launcelot budge not, budge says the
fiend, budge not says my conscience, conscience say I you   5
counsel well, fiend say I you counsel well, to be rul'd by
my conscience I should stay with the Jew my master,
(who God bless the mark) is a kind of devil; and to run
away from the Jew I should be ruled by the fiend, who
saving your reverence is the devil himself: certainly the   10
Jew is the very devil incarnation, and in my conscience,
my conscience is but a kind of hard conscience, to offer
to counsel me to stay with the Jew; the fiend gives the
more friendly counsel: I will run fiend, my heels are at
your commandment, I will run.   15

Enter Old Gobbo with a basket.

OLD GOBBO: Master young-man, you I pray you, which
    is the way to Master Jew's?

LAUNCELOT: O heavens, this is my true begotten Father,
    who being more than sand blind, high gravel blind,   20
    knows me not, I will try confusions with him.

OLD GOBBO: Master young gentleman, I pray you which
    is the way to Master Jew's?

LAUNCELOT: Turn up on your right hand at the next turn-
    ing, but at the next turning of all on your left; marry at   25
    the very next turning, turn of no hand, but turn down
    indirectly to the Jew's house.

OLD GOBBO: Be God's sonties 'twill be a hard way to hit,
    can you tell me whether one Launcelot that dwells with
    him, dwell with him or no.   30

LAUNCELOT: Talk of young Master Launcelot, mark me
    now, now will I raise the waters; talk you of young
    Master Launcelot?

OLD GOBBO: No Master, sir, but a poor man's son, his
Father though I say 't is an honest exceeding poor man,
and God be thanked well to live.

LAUNCELOT: Well, let his Father be what a' will, we talk
5   of young Master Launcelot.

OLD GOBBO: Your worship's friend and Launcelot.

LAUNCELOT: But I pray you *ergo* old man, *ergo* I beseech
you, talk you of young Master Launcelot?

OLD GOBBO: Of Launcelot, an 't please your mastership.

10 LAUNCELOT: *Ergo* Master Launcelot, talk not of Master
Launcelot Father, for the young gentleman according to
fates and destinies, and such odd sayings, the sisters three,
and such branches of learning, is indeed deceased, or as
you would say in plain terms, gone to heaven.

15 OLD GOBBO: Marry God forbid, the boy was the very
staff of my age, my very prop.

LAUNCELOT: Do I look like a cudgel or a hovel-post, a
staff or a prop: do you know me Father?

OLD GOBBO: Alack the day, I know you not young gentle-
20   man, but I pray you tell me, is my boy God rest his soul
alive or dead?

LAUNCELOT: Do you not know me Father?

OLD GOBBO: Alack sir I am sand blind, I know you
not.

25 LAUNCELOT: Nay, indeed if you had your eyes you might
fail of the knowing me: it is a wise Father that knows his
own child. Well, old man, I will tell you news of your
son, give me your blessing, truth will come to light,
murder cannot be hid long, a man's son may, but in the
30   end truth will out.

OLD GOBBO: Pray you sir stand up, I am sure you are not
Launcelot my boy.

LAUNCELOT: Pray you let's have no more fooling about

it, but give me your blessing: I am Launcelot your boy
that was, your son that is, your child that shall be.

OLD GOBBO: I cannot think you are my son.

LAUNCELOT: I know not what I shall think of that: but I
am Launcelot the Jew's man, and I am sure Margery your   5
wife is my mother.

OLD GOBBO: Her name is Margery indeed. I'll be sworn
if thou be Launcelot, thou art mine own flesh and blood:
Lord worshipp'd might he be, what a beard hast thou
got; thou hast got more hair on thy chin, than Dobbin   10
my fill-horse has on his tail.

LAUNCELOT: It should seem then that Dobbin's tail grows
backward. I am sure he had more hair of his tail than I
have of my face when I last saw him.

OLD GOBBO: Lord how art thou chang'd: how dost thou   15
and thy Master agree, I have brought him a present; how
gree you now?

LAUNCELOT: Well, well, but for mine own part, as I have
set up my rest to run away, so I will not rest till I have
run some ground; my Master's a very Jew, give him a   20
present, give him a halter, I am famish'd in his service.
You may tell every finger I have with my ribs: Father I
am glad you are come, give me your present to one
Master Bassanio, who indeed gives rare new liveries, if I
serve not him, I will run as far as God has any ground. O   25
rare fortune, here comes the man, to him Father, for I am
a Jew if I serve the Jew any longer.

Enter Bassanio with a follower or two.

BASSANIO: You may do so, but let it be so hasted that
supper be ready at the farthest by five of the clock: see   30
these letters delivered, put the liveries to making, and
desire Gratiano to come anon to my lodging.

Exit a Servant.

LAUNCELOT: To him father.

OLD GOBBO: God bless your worship.

BASSANIO: Gramercy, wouldst thou aught with me?

OLD GOBBO: Here's my son sir, a poor boy.

5 LAUNCELOT: Not a poor boy sir, but the rich Jew's man
that would sir as my Father shall specify.

OLD GOBBO: He hath a great infection sir, as one would
say to serve.

LAUNCELOT: Indeed the short and the long is, I serve the
10 Jew, and have a desire as my Father shall specify.

OLD GOBBO: His Master and he (saving your worship's
reverence) are scarce cater-cousins.

LAUNCELOT: To be brief, the very truth is, that the Jew
having done me wrong, doth cause me as my Father be-
15 ing I hope an old man shall frutify unto you.

OLD GOBBO: I have here a dish of doves that I would
bestow upon your worship, and my suit is —

LAUNCELOT: In very brief, the suit is impertinent to myself, as your worship shall know by this honest old man,
20 and though I say it, though old man, yet poor man my
Father.

BASSANIO: One speak for both, what would you?

LAUNCELOT: Serve you sir.

OLD GOBBO: That is the very defect of the matter sir.

25 BASSANIO: I know thee well, thou hast obtain'd thy suit,
Shylock thy master spoke with me this day,
And hath preferr'd thee, if it be preferment
To leave a rich Jew's service, to become
The follower of so poor a Gentleman.

30 LAUNCELOT: The old proverb is very well parted between
my Master Shylock and you sir, you have the grace of
God sir, and he hath enough.

BASSANIO: Thou speak'st it well; go father with thy son,

Take leave of thy old Master, and inquire
My lodging out; give him a livery
More guarded than his fellows': see it done.

LAUNCELOT: Father in, I cannot get a service, no, I have
ne'er a tongue in my head, well: if any man in Italy have 5
a fairer table which doth offer to swear upon a book, I
shall have good fortune; go to, here's a simple line of
life, here's a small trifle of wives, alas, fifteen wives is
nothing, eleven widows and nine maids is a simple coming in for one man, and then to 'scape drowning thrice, 10
and to be in peril of my life with the edge of a feather-
bed, here are simple scapes: well, if Fortune be a woman,
she's a good wench for this gear: Father come, I'll take
my leave of the Jew in the twinkling.

Exeunt Clown and old Gobbo. 15

BASSANIO: I pray thee good Leonardo think on this,
These things being bought and orderly bestowed
Return in haste, for I do feast tonight
My best esteem'd acquaintance, hie thee go.

LEONARDO: My best endeavours shall be done herein. 20

Enter Gratiano.

GRATIANO: Where's your Master?

LEONARDO: Yonder sir he walks.

Exit Leonardo.

GRATIANO: Signior Bassanio. 25

BASSANIO: Gratiano.

GRATIANO: I have a suit to you.

BASSANIO: You have obtain'd it.

GRATIANO: You must not deny me, I must go with you to
Belmont. 30

BASSANIO: Why then you must: but hear thee Gratiano,
Thou art too wild, too rude, and bold of voice,
Parts that become thee happily enough,

And in such eyes as ours appear not faults;
But where they are not known, why there they show
Something too liberal, pray thee take pain
To allay with some cold drops of modesty
5   Thy skipping spirit, lest through thy wild behaviour
I be misconster'd in the place I go to,
And lose my hopes.

GRATIANO: Signior Bassanio, hear me,
If I do not put on a sober habit,
10   Talk with respect, and swear but now and then,
Wear prayer books in my pocket, look demurely,
Nay more, while grace is saying hood mine eyes
Thus with my hat, and sigh and say Amen:
Use all the observance of civility
15   Like one well studied in a sad ostent
To please his Grandam, never trust me more.

BASSANIO: Well, we shall see your bearing.

GRATIANO: Nay but I bar tonight, you shall not gauge me
By what we do tonight.

20 BASSANIO: No that were pity,
I would entreat you rather to put on
Your boldest suit of mirth, for we have friends
That purpose merriment: but fare you well,
I have some business.

25 GRATIANO: And I must to Lorenzo and the rest,
But we will visit you at supper-time.

Exeunt.

II. 3

Enter Jessica and the Clown.

30 JESSICA: I am sorry thou wilt leave my father so,
Our house is hell, and thou a merry devil

Didst rob it of some taste of tediousness;
But fare thee well, there is a ducat for thee,
And Launcelot, soon at supper shalt thou see
Lorenzo, who is thy new Master's guest,
Give him this letter, do it secretly,   5
And so farewell: I would not have my Father
See me in talk with thee.

LAUNCELOT: Adieu, tears exhibit my tongue, most beautiful pagan, most sweet Jew, if a Christian do not play
the knave and get thee, I am much deceived; but adieu,   10
these foolish drops do somewhat drown my manly
spirit: adieu.

Exit.

JESSICA: Farewell good Launcelot.
Alack, what heinous sin is it in me   15
To be ashamed to be my Father's child,
But though I am a daughter to his blood,
I am not to his manners: O Lorenzo,
If thou keep promise I shall end this strife,
Become a Christian, and thy loving wife.   20

Exit.

II. 4

Enter Gratiano, Lorenzo, Salarino, and Solanio.

LORENZO: Nay, we will slink away in supper time,
Disguise us at my lodging, and return all in an hour.   25

GRATIANO: We have not made good preparation.

SALARINO: We have not spoke us yet of torch-bearers.

SOLANIO: 'Tis vile unless it may be quaintly ordered,
And better in my mind not undertook.

LORENZO: 'Tis now but four of clock, we have two   30
hours

To furnish us; friend Launcelot what's the news.

Enter Launcelot, with a letter.

LAUNCELOT: And it shall please you to break up this, it
　shall seem to signify.

5 LORENZO: I know the hand, in faith 'tis a fair hand,
　And whiter than the paper it writ on,
　Is the fair hand that writ.

GRATIANO: Love news in faith.

LAUNCELOT: By your leave sir.

10 LORENZO: Whither goest thou?

LAUNCELOT: Marry sir to bid my old Master the Jew to
　sup tonight with my new Master the Christian.

LORENZO: Hold here, take this, tell gentle Jessica
　I will not fail her, speak it privately:

15 Go Gentlemen, will you prepare you for this Masque to-
　night,
　I am provided of a torch-bearer.

Exit Clown.

SALARINO: Ay marry, I'll be gone about it straight.

20 SOLANIO: And so will I.

LORENZO: Meet me and Gratiano at Gratiano's lodging
　Some hour hence.

SALARINO: 'Tis good we do so.

Exeunt Salarino and Solanio.

25 GRATIANO: Was not that letter from fair Jessica?

LORENZO: I must needs tell thee all, she hath directed
　How I shall take her from her Father's house,
　What gold and jewels she is furnish'd with,
　What page's suit she hath in readiness:

30 If e'er the Jew her Father come to heaven,
　It will be for his gentle daughter's sake;
　And never dare misfortune cross her foot,
　Unless she do it under this excuse,

That she is issue to a faithless Jew:
Come go with me, peruse this as thou goest,
Fair Jessica shall be my torch-bearer.
Exeunt.

II. 5

Enter Shylock and his man that was the Clown.

SHYLOCK: Well, thou shalt see, thy eyes shall be thy judge,
The difference of old Shylock and Bassanio;
What Jessica, thou shalt not gormandise
As thou hast done with me: what Jessica?
And sleep, and snore, and rend apparel out.
Why Jessica I say.

LAUNCELOT: Why Jessica.

SHYLOCK: Who bids thee call? I do not bid thee call.

LAUNCELOT: Your worship was wont to tell me
I could do nothing without bidding.

Enter Jessica.

JESSICA: Call you? what is your will?

SHYLOCK: I am bid forth to supper Jessica,
There are my keys: but wherefore should I go?
I am not bid for love, they flatter me,
But yet I'll go in hate, to feed upon
The prodigal Christian. Jessica my girl,
Look to my house, I am right loath to go,
There is some ill a-brewing towards my rest,
For I did dream of money-bags tonight.

LAUNCELOT: I beseech you sir go, my young Master doth
expect your reproach.

SHYLOCK: So do I his.

LAUNCELOT: And they have conspired together, I will not
say you shall see a Masque, but if you do, then it was

not for nothing that my nose fell a-bleeding on Black
Monday last, at six o'clock i' th' morning, falling out
that year on Ash Wednesday was four year in th' afternoon.

5 SHYLOCK: What are there masques? hear you me Jessica,
Lock up my doors, and when you hear the drum
And the vile squealing of the wry-neck'd fife,
Clamber not you up to the casements then,
Nor thrust your head into the public street
10 To gaze on Christian fools with varnish'd faces:
But stop my house's ears, I mean my casements,
Let not the sound of shallow foppery enter
My sober house. By Jacob's staff I swear
I have no mind of feasting forth tonight:
15 But I will go: go you before me sirrah,
Say I will come.

LAUNCELOT: I will go before sir.
Mistress look out at window for all this;
There will come a Christian by,
20 Will be worth a Jew's eye.
                                             Exit.
SHYLOCK: What says that fool of Hagar's offspring? ha.
JESSICA: His words were farewell mistress, nothing else.
SHYLOCK: The patch is kind enough, but a huge feeder:
25 Snail-slow in profit, and he sleeps by day
More than the wild-cat: drones hive not with me,
Therefore I part with him, and part with him
To one that I would have him help to waste
His borrowed purse. Well Jessica go in,
30 Perhaps I will return immediately;
Do as I bid you, shut doors after you, fast bind, fast find,
A proverb never stale in thrifty mind.
                                             Exit.

JESSICA: Farewell, and if my fortune be not crost,
  I have a Father, you a daughter lost.
                    Exit.

II. 6

      Enter the Masquers, Gratiano and Salarino.   5
GRATIANO: This is the pent-house under which Lorenzo
  Desired us to make stand.
SALARINO: His hour is almost past.
GRATIANO: And it is marvel he out-dwells his hour,
  For lovers ever run before the clock.   10
SALARINO: O ten times faster Venus' pigeons fly
  To seal love's bonds new-made, than they are wont
  To keep obliged faith unforfeited.
GRATIANO: That ever holds: who riseth from a feast
  With that keen appetite that he sits down?   15
  Where is the horse that doth untread again
  His tedious measures with the unbated fire,
  That he did pace them first: all things that are,
  Are with more spirit chased than enjoy'd.
  How like a younger or a prodigal   20
  The scarfed bark puts from her native bay,
  Hugg'd and embraced by the strumpet wind:
  How like the prodigal doth she return
  With over-weather'd ribs and ragged sails,
  Lean, rent, and beggar'd by the strumpet wind?   25
                   Enter Lorenzo.
SALARINO: Here comes Lorenzo, more of this hereafter.
LORENZO: Sweet friends, your patience for my long abode,
  Not I, but my affairs have made you wait:
  When you shall please to play the thieves for wives   30
  I'll watch as long for you then: approach,

Here dwells my father Jew. Hoa, who's within?
Enter Jessica above, in boy's clothes.

JESSICA: Who are you? tell me for more certainty,
Albeit I 'll swear that I do know your tongue.

5 LORENZO: Lorenzo, and thy love.

JESSICA: Lorenzo certain, and my love indeed,
For who love I so much? and now who knows
But you Lorenzo, whether I am yours?

LORENZO: Heaven and thy thoughts are witness that thou
10   art.

JESSICA: Here, catch this casket, it is worth the pains,
I am glad 'tis night, you do not look on me,
For I am much asham'd of my exchange:
But love is blind, and lovers cannot see
15   The pretty follies that themselves commit,
For if they could, Cupid himself would blush
To see me thus transformed to a boy.

LORENZO: Descend, for you must be my torch-bearer.

JESSICA: What, must I hold a candle to my shames?
20   They in themselves good sooth are too too light.
Why, 'tis an office of discovery love,
And I should be obscur'd.

LORENZO: So are you sweet,
Even in the lovely garnish of a boy: but come at once,
25   For the close night doth play the run-away,
And we are stay'd for at Bassanio's feast.

JESSICA: I will make fast the doors and gild myself
With some more ducats, and be with you straight.
Exit above.

30 GRATIANO: Now by my hood, a gentle, and no Jew.

LORENZO: Beshrew me but I love her heartily.
For she is wise, if I can judge of her,
And fair she is, if that mine eyes be true,

And true she is, as she hath prov'd herself:
And therefore like herself, wise, fair, and true,
Shall she be placed in my constant soul.
                   Enter Jessica.
What, art thou come? on gentlemen, away,   5
Our masquing mates by this time for us stay.
          Exit with Jessica and Salarino.
                Enter Antonio.

ANTONIO: Who 's there?
GRATIANO: Signior Antonio?   10
ANTONIO: Fie, fie, Gratiano, where are all the rest?
'Tis nine o'clock, our friends all stay for you,
No masque tonight, the wind is come about,
Bassanio presently will go aboard,
I have sent twenty out to seek for you.   15
GRATIANO: I am glad on 't, I desire no more delight
Than to be under sail, and gone tonight.
                 Exeunt.

II. 7

   Enter Portia with Morocco, and both their trains.   20
PORTIA: Go, draw aside the curtains, and discover
The several caskets to this noble Prince:
Now make your choice.
MOROCCO: The first of gold, who this inscription bears,
Who chooseth me, shall gain what many men desire.   25
The second silver, which this promise carries,
Who chooseth me, shall get as much as he deserves.
This third, dull lead, with warning all as blunt,
Who chooseth me, must give and hazard all he hath.
How shall I know if I do choose the right?   30
PORTIA: The one of them contains my picture Prince,

If you choose that, then I am yours withal.

MOROCCO: Some God direct my judgement, let me see,
I will survey the inscriptions, back again:
What says this leaden casket?
5 Who chooseth me, must give and hazard all he hath.
Must give, for what? for lead, hazard for lead?
This casket threatens; men that hazard all
Do it in hope of fair advantages:
A golden mind stoops not to shows of dross,
10 I'll then nor give nor hazard aught for lead.
What says the silver with her virgin hue?
Who chooseth me, shall get as much as he deserves.
As much as he deserves; pause there Morocco,
And weigh thy value with an even hand,
15 If thou be'st rated by thy estimation
Thou dost deserve enough, and yet enough
May not extend so far as to the Lady:
And yet to be afear'd of my deserving,
Were but a weak disabling of myself.
20 As much as I deserve, why that's the Lady.
I do in birth deserve her, and in fortunes,
In graces, and in qualities of breeding:
But more than these, in love I do deserve.
What if I stray'd no farther, but chose here?
25 Let's see once more this saying grav'd in gold.
Who chooseth me shall gain what many men desire:
Why that's the Lady, all the world desires her:
From the four corners of the earth they come
To kiss this shrine, this mortal breathing Saint.
30 The Hyrcanian deserts, and the vasty wilds
Of wide Arabia are as throughfares now
For Princes to come view fair Portia.
The watery Kingdom, whose ambitious head

Spets in the face of heaven, is no bar
To stop the foreign spirits, but they come
As o'er a brook to see fair Portia.
One of these three contains her heavenly picture.
Is 't like that lead contains her? 'twere damnation   5
To think so base a thought, it were too gross
To rib her cerecloth in the obscure grave:
Or shall I think in silver she's immur'd
Being ten times undervalued to tried gold;
O sinful thought, never so rich a gem   10
Was set in worse than gold! They have in England
A coin that bears the figure of an Angel
Stamp'd in gold, but that 's insculp'd upon:
But here an Angel in a golden bed
Lies all within. Deliver me the key: 15
Here do I choose, and thrive I as I may.

PORTIA: There take it Prince, and if my form lie there
    Then I am yours.

MOROCCO: O hell! what have we here, a carrion death,
    Within whose empty eye there is a written scroll;   20
    I'll read the writing.

> *All that glisters is not gold,*
> *Often have you heard that told;*
> *Many a man his life hath sold*
> *But my outside to behold;*   25
> *Gilded tombs do worms infold:*
> *Had you been as wise as bold,*
> *Young in limbs, in judgement old,*
> *Your answer had not been inscroll'd,*
> *Fare you well, your suit is cold.*   30

MOROCCO: Cold indeed, and labour lost,
    Then farewell heat, and welcome frost:
    Portia adieu, I have too griev'd a heart

To take a tedious leave: thus losers part.

Exit.

PORTIA: A gentle riddance: draw the curtains, go.
Let all of his complexion choose me so.

5   *Exeunt. Flourish cornets.*

II. 8

Enter Salarino and Solanio.

SALARINO: Why man I saw Bassanio under sail;
With him is Gratiano gone along;
10   And in their ship I am sure Lorenzo is not.

SOLANIO: The villain Jew with outcries rais'd the Duke,
Who went with him to search Bassanio's ship.

SALARINO: He came too late, the ship was under sail;
But there the Duke was given to understand
15   That in a gondilo were seen together
Lorenzo and his amorous Jessica.
Besides, Antonio certified the Duke
They were not with Bassanio in his ship.

SOLANIO: I never heard a passion so confus'd,
20   So strange, outrageous, and so variable,
As the dog Jew did utter in the streets;
My daughter, O my ducats, O my daughter,
Fled with a Christian, O my Christian ducats!
Justice, the law, my ducats, and my daughter;
25   A sealed bag, two sealed bags of ducats,
Of double ducats, stolen from me by my daughter,
And jewels, two stones, two rich and precious stones,
Stolen by my daughter: justice, find the girl,
She hath the stones upon her, and the ducats.

30 SALARINO: Why all the boys in Venice follow him,
Crying his stones, his daughter, and his ducats.

SOLANIO: Let good Antonio look he keep his day
  Or he shall pay for this.
SALARINO: Marry well remember'd;
  I reason'd with a Frenchman yesterday,
  Who told me, in the narrow seas that part   5
  The French and English, there miscarried
  A vessel of our country richly fraught:
  I thought upon Antonio when he told me,
  And wish'd in silence that it were not his.
SOLANIO: You were best to tell Antonio what you hear. 10
  Yet do not suddenly, for it may grieve him.
SALARINO: A kinder Gentleman treads not the earth,
  I saw Bassanio and Antonio part,
  Bassanio told him he would make some speed
  Of his return: he answer'd, do not so,   15
  Slubber not business for my sake Bassanio,
  But stay the very riping of the time,
  And for the Jew's bond which he hath of me,
  Let it not enter in your mind of love:
  Be merry, and employ your chiefest thoughts 20
  To courtship, and such fair ostents of love
  As shall conveniently become you there;
  And even there his eye being big with tears,
  Turning his face, he put his hand behind him,
  And with affection wondrous sensible   25
  He wrung Bassanio's hand, and so they parted.
SOLANIO: I think he only loves the world for him,
  I pray thee let us go and find him out
  And quicken his embraced heaviness
  With some delight or other.   30
SALARINO: Do we so.

           Exeunt.

II. 9

Enter Nerissa and a Servitor.

NERISSA: Quick, quick I pray thee, draw the curtain straight,

5   The Prince of Arragon hath ta'en his oath,
And comes to his election presently.

Enter Arragon, his train, and Portia. Flourish cornets.

PORTIA: Behold, there stand the caskets noble Prince,
If you choose that wherein I am contain'd,

10   Straight shall our nuptial rites be solemniz'd:
But if you fail, without more speech my Lord,
You must be gone from hence immediately.

ARRAGON: I am enjoin'd by oath to observe three things;
First, never to unfold to any one

15   Which casket 'twas I chose; next, if I fail
Of the right casket, never in my life
To woo a maid in way of marriage:
Lastly, if I do fail in fortune of my choice,
Immediately to leave you, and be gone.

20 PORTIA: To these injunctions every one doth swear
That comes to hazard for my worthless self.

ARRAGON: And so have I address'd me, fortune now
To my heart's hope: gold, silver, and base lead.
Who chooseth me must give and hazard all he hath.

25   You shall look fairer ere I give or hazard.
What says the golden chest, ha, let me see:
Who chooseth me, shall gain what many men desire:
What many men desire, that many may be meant
By the fool multitude that choose by show,

30   Not learning more than the fond eye doth teach,
Which pries not to th' interior, but like the martlet

Builds in the weather on the outward wall,
Even in the force and road of casualty.
I will not choose what many men desire,
Because I will not jump with common spirits,
And rank me with the barbarous multitudes.   5
Why then to thee thou silver treasure house,
Tell me once more, what title thou dost bear;
Who chooseth me shall get as much as he deserves:
And well said too; for who shall go about
To cozen Fortune, and be honourable   10
Without the stamp of merit, let none presume
To wear an undeserved dignity:
O that estates, degrees, and offices,
Were not deriv'd corruptly, and that clear honour
Were purchas'd by the merit of the wearer;   15
How many then should cover that stand bare?
How many be commanded that command?
How much low peasantry would then be gleaned
From the true seed of honour? And how much honour
Pick'd from the chaff and ruin of the times,   20
To be new varnish'd: Well, but to my choice.
Who chooseth me shall get as much as he deserves.
I will assume desert; give me a key for this,
And instantly unlock my fortunes here.

PORTIA: Too long a pause for that which you find there.   25

ARRAGON: What 's here, the portrait of a blinking idiot
  Presenting me a schedule, I will read it:
  How much unlike art thou to Portia!
  How much unlike my hopes and my deservings!
  Who chooseth me, shall have as much as he deserves.   30
  Did I deserve no more than a fool's head,
  Is that my prize, are my deserts no better?

PORTIA: To offend and judge are distinct offices,

And of opposed natures.

ARRAGON: What is here?
    The fire seven times tried this,
    Seven times tried that judgement is,
5   *That did never choose amiss,*
    Some there be that shadows kiss,
    Such have but a shadow's bliss:
    There be fools alive I wis
    Silver'd o'er, and so was this:
10   *Take what wife you will to bed,*
    I will ever be your head:
    So be gone, you are sped.
  Still more fool I shall appear
  By the time I linger here,
15 With one fool's head I came to woo,
  But I go away with two.
  Sweet adieu, I'll keep my oath,
  Patiently to bear my wroth.
      Exeunt Arragon and train.
20 PORTIA: Thus hath the candle sing'd the moth:
  O these deliberate fools when they do choose,
  They have the wisdom by their wit to lose.
 NERISSA: The ancient saying is no heresy,
  Hanging and wiving goes by destiny.
25 PORTIA: Come draw the curtain Nerissa.
      Enter Messenger.
 MESSENGER: Where is my Lady?
 PORTIA: Here, what would my Lord?
 MESSENGER: Madam, there is alighted at your gate
30 A young Venetian, one that comes before
  To signify th' approaching of his Lord,
  From whom he bringeth sensible regrets;
  To wit (besides commends and courteous breath)

Gifts of rich value; yet I have not seen
So likely an Ambassador of love.
A day in April never came so sweet
To show how costly summer was at hand,
As this fore-spurrer comes before his Lord.   5

PORTIA: No more I pray thee, I am half afeard
Thou wilt say anon he is some kin to thee,
Thou spend'st such high-day wit in praising him:
Come, come Nerissa, for I long to see
Quick Cupid's post, that comes so mannerly.   10

NERISSA: Bassanio Lord, love if thy will it be.

Exeunt.

III. 1

Enter Solanio and Salarino.

SOLANIO: Now, what news on the Rialto?   15

SALARINO: Why yet it lives there uncheck'd, that Antonio
hath a ship of rich lading wrack'd on the Narrow Seas;
the Goodwins I think they call the place, a very dangerous flat, and fatal, where the carcases of many a tall ship,
lie buried, as they say, if my gossip Report be an honest   20
woman of her word.

SOLANIO: I would she were as lying a gossip in that, as
ever knapp'd ginger, or made her neighbours believe she
wept for the death of a third husband: but it is true, without any slips of prolixity, or crossing the plain high-way 25
of talk, that the good Antonio, the honest Antonio; O
that I had a title good enough to keep his name company!

SALARINO: Come, the full stop.

SOLANIO: Ha, what sayest thou, why the end is, he hath   30
lost a ship.

SALARINO: I would it might prove the end of his losses.

SOLANIO: Let me say Amen betimes, lest the devil cross my prayer, for here he comes in the likeness of a Jew. How now Shylock, what news among the merchants?

5   *Enter Shylock.*

SHYLOCK: You knew none so well, none so well as you, of my daughter's flight.

SALARINO: That's certain, I for my part knew the tailor that made the wings she flew withal.

10 **SOLANIO:** And Shylock for his own part knew the bird was fledg'd, and then it is the complexion of them all to leave the dam.

SHYLOCK: She is damn'd for it.

SALARINO: That's certain, if the devil may be her judge.

15 **SHYLOCK:** My own flesh and blood to rebel.

SOLANIO: Out upon it old carrion, rebels it at these years?

SHYLOCK: I say my daughter is my flesh and blood.

SALARINO: There is more difference between thy flesh and hers, than between jet and ivory, more between your

20   bloods, than there is between red wine and rhenish: but tell us, do you hear whether Antonio have had any loss at sea or no?

SHYLOCK: There I have another bad match, a bankrout, a prodigal, who dare scarce show his head on the Rialto, a

25   beggar that was us'd to come so smug upon the Mart: let him look to his bond, he was wont to call me usurer, let him look to his bond, he was wont to lend money for a Christian courtesy, let him look to his bond.

SALARINO: Why I am sure if he forfeit, thou wilt not take

30   his flesh, what's that good for?

SHYLOCK: To bait fish withal, if it will feed nothing else, it will feed my revenge; he hath disgrac'd me, and hinder'd me half a million, laugh'd at my losses, mock'd at my gains, scorned my Nation, thwarted my bargains, cooled my friends, heated mine enemies, and what 's his reason? I am a Jew: hath not a Jew eyes? hath not a Jew hands, organs, dimensions, senses, affections, passions, fed with the same food, hurt with the same weapons, subject 5 to the same diseases, healed by the same means, warmed and cooled by the same winter and summer as a Christian is: if you prick us do we not bleed? if you tickle us do we not laugh? if you poison us do we not die? and if you wrong us shall we not revenge? if we are like you in the 10 rest, we will resemble you in that. If a Jew wrong a Christian, what is his humility, revenge! If a Christian wrong a Jew, what should his sufferance be by Christian example, why revenge! The villainy you teach me I will execute, and it shall go hard but I will better the instruc- 15 tion.

Enter a man from Antonio.

SERVANT: Gentlemen, my master Antonio is at his house, and desires to speak with you both.

SALARINO: We have been up and down to seek him.   20

Enter Tubal.

SOLANIO: Here comes another of the Tribe, a third cannot be match'd, unless the devil himself turn Jew.

Exeunt Gentlemen.

SHYLOCK: How now Tubal, what news from Genoa? hast 25 thou found my daughter?

TUBAL: I often came where I did hear of her, but cannot find her.

SHYLOCK: Why there, there, there, there, a diamond gone cost me two thousand ducats in Frankfort, the curse never 30 fell upon our Nation till now, I never felt it till now, two thousand ducats in that, and other precious, precious jewels: I would my daughter were dead at my foot, and the jewels

in her ear: would she were hears'd at my foot, and the
ducats in her coffin: no news of them, why so? and I
know not how much is spent in the search: why thou
loss upon loss, the thief gone with so much, and so much
5 to find the thief, and no satisfaction, no revenge, nor no
ill luck stirring but what lights a' my shoulders, no sighs
but a' my breathing, no tears but a' my shedding.

TUBAL: Yes, other men have ill luck too, Antonio as I
heard in Genoa!

10 SHYLOCK: What, what, what, ill luck, ill luck.

TUBAL: Hath an argosy cast away coming from Tripolis.

SHYLOCK: I thank God, I thank God, is it true, is it true?

TUBAL: I spoke with some of the sailors that escaped the
wrack.

15 SHYLOCK: I thank thee good Tubal, good news, good
news: ha, ha, here in Genoa.

TUBAL: Your daughter spent in Genoa, as I heard, one
night fourscore ducats.

SHYLOCK: Thou stick'st a dagger in me, I shall never see
20 my gold again, fourscore ducats at a sitting, fourscore
ducats.

TUBAL: There came divers of Antonio's creditors in my
company to Venice, that swear he cannot choose but
break.

25 SHYLOCK: I am very glad of it, I'll plague him, I'll torture
him, I am glad of it.

TUBAL: One of them showed me a ring that he had of your
daughter for a monkey.

SHYLOCK: Out upon her, thou torturest me Tubal, it was
30 my turkis, I had it of Leah when I was a bachelor: I would
not have given it for a wilderness of monkeys.

TUBAL: But Antonio is certainly undone.

SHYLOCK: Nay, that's true, that's very true, go Tubal, fee

me an Officer, bespeak him a fortnight before, I will have
the heart of him if he forfeit, for were he out of Venice,
I can make what merchandise I will: go Tubal, and meet
me at our Synagogue, go good Tubal, at our Synagogue
Tubal.   5

Exeunt.

III. 2

Enter Bassanio, Portia, Gratiano, Nerissa, and all their train.

PORTIA: I pray you tarry, pause a day or two
  Before you hazard, for in choosing wrong   10
  I lose your company; therefore forbear awhile,
  There's something tells me (but it is not love)
  I would not lose you, and you know yourself,
  Hate counsels not in such a quality;
  But lest you should not understand me well,   15
  And yet a maiden hath no tongue, but thought,
  I would detain you here some month or two
  Before you venture for me. I could teach you
  How to choose right, but then I am forsworn,
  So will I never be, so may you miss me,   20
  But if you do, you'll make me wish a sin,
  That I had been forsworn: Beshrew your eyes,
  They have o'er-look'd me and divided me,
  One half of me is yours, the other half yours,
  Mine own I would say: but if mine then yours,   25
  And so all yours; O these naughty times
  Puts bars between the owners and their rights.
  And so though yours, not yours (prove it so)
  Let Fortune go to hell for it, not I.
  I speak too long, but 'tis to peize the time,   30
  To eke it, and to draw it out in length,

To stay you from election.

BASSANIO: Let me choose,
    For as I am, I live upon the rack.

PORTIA: Upon the rack Bassanio, then confess
5   What treason there is mingled with your love.

BASSANIO: None but that ugly treason of mistrust,
    Which makes me fear the enjoying of my love:
    There may as well be amity and life,
    'Tween snow and fire, as treason and my love.

10 PORTIA: Ay, but I fear you speak upon the rack,
    Where men enforced do speak any thing.

BASSANIO: Promise me life, and I'll confess the truth.

PORTIA: Well then, confess and live.

BASSANIO: Confess and love
15   Had been the very sum of my confession:
    O happy torment, when my torturer
    Doth teach me answers for deliverance:
    But let me to my fortune and the caskets.

PORTIA: Away then, I am lock'd in one of them,
20   If you do love me, you will find me out.
    Nerissa and the rest, stand all aloof,
    Let music sound while he doth make his choice,
    Then if he lose he makes a swan-like end,
    Fading in music. That the comparison
25   May stand more proper, my eye shall be the stream
    And watery death-bed for him: he may win,
    And what is music then? Then music is
    Even as the flourish, when true subjects bow
    To a new crowned Monarch: Such it is,
30   As are those dulcet sounds in break of day,
    That creep into the dreaming bridegroom's ear,
    And summon him to marriage. Now he goes
    With no less presence, but with much more love

Than young Alcides, when he did redeem
The virgin tribute, paid by howling Troy
To the Sea-monster: I stand for sacrifice,
The rest aloof are the Dardanian wives:
With bleared visages come forth to view   5
The issue of th' exploit: Go Hercules,
Live thou, I live; with much much more dismay
I view the fight, than thou that mak'st the fray.

Here music.

A Song the whilst Bassanio comments on the caskets to himself.   10

> *Tell me where is fancy bred,*
> *Or in the heart, or in the head:*
> *How begot, how nourished?*   *Reply, reply.*
> *It is engender'd in the eyes,*
> *With gazing fed, and Fancy dies,*   15
> *In the cradle where it lies:*
> *Let us all ring Fancy's knell.*
> *I'll begin it*
> *Ding, dong, bell.*

ALL: *Ding, dong, bell.*   20

BASSANIO: So may the outward shows be least themselves,
The world is still deceiv'd with ornament.
In Law, what plea so tainted and corrupt,
But being season'd with a gracious voice,
Obscures the show of evil? In Religion,   25
What damned error, but some sober brow
Will bless it, and approve it with a text,
Hiding the grossness with fair ornament:
There is no vice so simple, but assumes
Some mark of virtue on his outward parts;   30
How many cowards, whose hearts are all as false
As stairs of sand, wear yet upon their chins
The beards of Hercules and frowning Mars,

Who inward search'd, have livers white as milk,
And these assume but valour's excrement,
To render them redoubted. Look on beauty,
And you shall see 'tis purchas'd by the weight,
5   Which therein works a miracle in nature,
Making them lightest that wear most of it:
So are those crisped snaky golden locks
Which make such wanton gambols with the wind
Upon supposed fairness, often known
10 To be the dowry of a second head,
The skull that bred them in the sepulchre.
Thus ornament is but the guiled shore
To a most dangerous sea: the beauteous scarf
Veiling an Indian beauty; in a word,
15 The seeming truth which cunning times put on
To intrap the wisest. Therefore then thou gaudy gold,
Hard food for Midas, I will none of thee,
Nor none of thee thou pale and common drudge
'Tween man and man: but thou, thou meagre lead
20 Which rather threat'nest than dost promise aught,
Thy paleness moves me more than eloquence,
And here choose I, joy be the consequence.
PORTIA: How all the other passions fleet to air,
As doubtful thoughts, and rash-embrac'd despair:
25 And shuddering fear, and green-eyed jealousy.
O love be moderate, allay thy ecstasy,
In measure rain thy joy, scant this excess,
I feel too much thy blessing, make it less,
For fear I surfeit.
30 BASSANIO: What find I here?
Fair Portia's counterfeit. What demi-God
Hath come so near creation? move these eyes?
Or whether riding on the balls of mine

Seem they in motion? Here are sever'd lips
Parted with sugar breath, so sweet a bar
Should sunder such sweet friends: here in her hairs
The painter plays the spider, and hath woven
A golden mesh t' intrap the hearts of men   5
Faster than gnats in cobwebs: but her eyes,
How could he see to do them? having made one,
Methinks it should have power to steal both his
And leave itself unfurnish'd: Yet look how far
The substance of my praise doth wrong this shadow   10
In underprizing it, so far this shadow
Doth limp behind the substance. Here's the scroll,
The continent, and summary of my fortune.

> *You that choose not by the view*
> *Chance as fair, and choose as true:*   15
> *Since this fortune falls to you,*
> *Be content, and seek no new.*
> *If you be well pleas'd with this,*
> *And hold your fortune for your bliss,*
> *Turn you where your Lady is,*   20
> *And claim her with a loving kiss.*

A gentle scroll: fair Lady, by your leave,
I come by note to give, and to receive,
Like one of two contending in a prize
That thinks he hath done well in people's eyes: 25
Hearing applause and universal shout,
Giddy in spirit, still gazing in a doubt
Whether those peals of praise be his or no.
So thrice fair Lady stand I even so,
As doubtful whether what I see be true,   30
Until confirm'd, sign'd, ratified by you.

PORTIA: You see me Lord Bassanio where I stand,
  Such as I am; though for myself alone

I would not be ambitious in my wish,
To wish myself much better, yet for you,
I would be trebled twenty times myself,
A thousand times more fair, ten thousand times
5   More rich, that only to stand high in your account,
I might in virtues, beauties, livings, friends,
Exceed account: but the full sum of me
Is sum of nothing: which to term in gross,
Is an unlessoned girl, unschool'd, unpractis'd,
10   Happy in this, she is not yet so old
But she may learn: happier than this,
She is not bred so dull but she can learn;
Happiest of all, is that her gentle spirit
Commits itself to yours to be directed,
15   As from her Lord, her Governor, her King.
Myself, and what is mine, to you and yours
Is now converted. But now I was the Lord
Of this fair mansion, master of my servants,
Queen o'er myself: and even now, but now,
20   This house, these servants, and this same myself
Are yours, my Lord, I give them with this ring,
Which when you part from, lose, or give away,
Let it presage the ruin of your love,
And be my vantage to exclaim on you.
25 BASSANIO: Madam, you have bereft me of all words,
Only my blood speaks to you in my veins,
And there is such confusion in my powers,
As after some oration fairly spoke
By a beloved Prince, there doth appear
30   Among the buzzing pleased multitude,
Where every something being blent together,
Turns to a wild of nothing, save of joy
Express'd, and not express'd: but when this ring

Parts from this finger, then parts life from hence,
O then be bold to say Bassanio's dead.
NERISSA: My Lord and Lady, it is now our time
That have stood by and seen our wishes prosper,
To cry good joy, good joy my Lord and Lady.   5
GRATIANO: My Lord Bassanio, and my gentle Lady,
I wish you all the joy that you can wish:
For I am sure you can wish none from me:
And when your Honours mean to solemnize
The bargain of your faith: I do beseech you   10
Even at that time I may be married too.
BASSANIO: With all my heart, so thou canst get a wife.
GRATIANO: I thank your Lordship, you have got me one.
My eyes my Lord can look as swift as yours:
You saw the mistress, I beheld the maid: 15
You lov'd, I lov'd for intermission,
No more pertains to me my Lord than you;
Your fortune stood upon the caskets there,
And so did mine too, as the matter falls:
For wooing here until I sweat again,   20
And swearing till my very roof was dry
With oaths of love, at last, if promise last,
I got a promise of this fair one here
To have her love: provided that your fortune
Achiev'd her mistress.   25
PORTIA: Is this true Nerissa?
NERISSA: Madam it is so, so you stand pleas'd withal.
BASSANIO: And do you Gratiano mean good faith?
GRATIANO: Yes faith my Lord.
BASSANIO: Our feast shall be much honoured in your   30
marriage.
GRATIANO: We 'll play with them the first boy for a
thousand ducats.

NERISSA: What and stake down?

GRATIANO: No, we shall ne'er win at that sport, and stake
down.
But who comes here? Lorenzo and his Infidel?
5   What and my old Venetian friend Salerio?
Enter Lorenzo, Jessica, and Salerio, a messenger from Venice.

BASSANIO: Lorenzo and Salerio, welcome hither,
If that the youth of my new interest here
Have power to bid you welcome: by your leave
10   I bid my very friends and countrymen
Sweet Portia welcome.

PORTIA: So do I my Lord, they are entirely welcome.

LORENZO: I thank your honour; for my part my Lord,
My purpose was not to have seen you here,
15   But meeting with Salerio by the way,
He did entreat me past all saying nay
To come with him along.

SALERIO: I did my Lord,
And I have reason for it, Signior Antonio
20   Commends him to you.

BASSANIO: Ere I ope his letter
I pray you tell me how my good friend doth.

SALERIO: Not sick my Lord, unless it be in mind,
Nor well, unless in mind: his letter there
25   Will show you his estate.
Bassanio opens the letter.

GRATIANO: Nerissa, cheer yon stranger, bid her welcome.
Your hand Salerio, what's the news from Venice?
How doth that royal merchant good Antonio?
30   I know he will be glad of our success,
We are the Jasons, we have won the fleece.

SALERIO: I would you had won the fleece that he hath
lost.

PORTIA: There are some shrewd contents in yond same paper,
   That steals the colour from Bassanio's cheek,
   Some dear friend dead, else nothing in the world
   Could turn so much the constitution
   Of any constant man. What, worse and worse?   5
   With leave Bassanio I am half yourself,
   And I must freely have the half of anything
   That this same paper brings you.
BASSANIO: O sweet Portia,
   Here are a few of the unpleasant'st words   10
   That ever blotted paper. Gentle Lady
   When I did first impart my love to you,
   I freely told you all the wealth I had
   Ran in my veins: I was a Gentleman,
   And then I told you true: and yet dear Lady,   15
   Rating myself at nothing, you shall see
   How much I was a braggart, when I told you
   My state was nothing, I should then have told you
   That I was worse than nothing: for indeed
   I have engag'd myself to a dear friend,   20
   Engag'd my friend to his mere enemy
   To feed my means. Here is a letter Lady,
   The paper as the body of my friend,
   And every word in it a gaping wound
   Issuing life blood. But is it true Salerio,   25
   Hath all his ventures fail'd, what not one hit,
   From Tripolis, from Mexico and England,
   From Lisbon, Barbary, and India,
   And not one vessel scape the dreadful touch
   Of merchant-marring rocks?   30
SALERIO: Not one my Lord.
   Besides, it should appear, that if he had
   The present money to discharge the Jew,

He would not take it: never did I know
A creature that did bear the shape of man
So keen and greedy to confound a man.
He plies the Duke at morning and at night,
5 And doth impeach the freedom of the state
If they deny him justice. Twenty merchants,
The Duke himself, and the Magnificoes
Of greatest port have all persuaded with him,
But none can drive him from the envious plea
10 Of forfeiture, of justice, and his bond.
JESSICA: When I was with him, I have heard him swear
To Tubal and to Chus, his countrymen,
That he would rather have Antonio's flesh,
Than twenty times the value of the sum
15 That he did owe him: and I know my Lord,
If law, authority, and power deny not,
It will go hard with poor Antonio.
PORTIA: Is it your dear friend that is thus in trouble?
BASSANIO: The dearest friend to me, the kindest man,
20 The best-condition'd, and unwearied spirit
In doing courtesies: and one in whom
The ancient Roman honour more appears
Than any that draws breath in Italy.
PORTIA: What sum owes he the Jew?
25 BASSANIO: For me three thousand ducats.
PORTIA: What, no more?
Pay him six thousand, and deface the bond:
Double six thousand, and then treble that,
Before a friend of this description
30 Shall lose a hair through Bassanio's fault.
First go with me to church, and call me wife,
And then away to Venice to your friend:
For never shall you lie by Portia's side

With an unquiet soul. You shall have gold
To pay the petty debt twenty times over.
When it is paid, bring your true friend along:
My maid Nerissa, and myself meantime
Will live as maids and widows; come away,   5
For you shall hence upon your wedding-day:
Bid your friends welcome, show a merry cheer,
Since you are dear bought, I will love you dear.
But let me hear the letter of your friend.

BASSANIO: *Sweet Bassanio, my ships have all miscarried, my*   10
creditors grow cruel, my estate is very low, my bond to the Jew
is forfeit, and since in paying it, it is impossible I should live,
all debts are clear'd between you and I, if I might but see you
at my death: notwithstanding, use your pleasure, if your love
do not persuade you to come, let not my letter.   15

PORTIA: O love! dispatch all business and be gone.

BASSANIO: Since I have your good leave to go away,
I will make haste; but till I come again,
No bed shall e'er be guilty of my stay,
No rest be interposer 'twixt us twain.   20

Exeunt.

III. 3

Enter the Jew and Solanio, and Antonio and the Gaoler.

SHYLOCK: Gaoler, look to him, tell not me of mercy,
This is the fool that lends out money gratis.   25
Gaoler, look to him.

ANTONIO: Hear me yet good Shylock.

SHYLOCK: I'll have my bond, speak not against my bond,
I have sworn an oath that I will have my bond:
Thou call'dst me dog before thou hadst a cause,   30
But since I am a dog, beware my fangs,

    The Duke shall grant me justice, I do wonder
    Thou naughty gaoler, that thou art so fond
    To come abroad with him at his request.
ANTONIO: I pray thee hear me speak.
5 SHYLOCK: I'll have my bond, I will not hear thee speak,
    I'll have my bond, and therefore speak no more.
    I'll not be made a soft and dull ey'd fool,
    To shake the head, relent, and sigh, and yield
    To Christian intercessors: follow not,
10   I'll have no speaking, I will have my bond.
                Exit Jew.
SOLANIO: It is the most impenetrable cur that ever kept
    with men.
ANTONIO: Let him alone,
15   I'll follow him no more with bootless prayers:
    He seeks my life, his reason well I know;
    I oft deliver'd from his forfeitures
    Many that have at times made moan to me,
    Therefore he hates me.
20 SOLANIO: I am sure the Duke will never grant this for-
    feiture to hold.
ANTONIO: The Duke cannot deny the course of law:
    For the commodity that strangers have
    With us in Venice, if it be denied,
25   Will much impeach the justice of the State,
    Since that the trade and profit of the city
    Consisteth of all Nations. Therefore go,
    These griefs and losses have so bated me,
    That I shall hardly spare a pound of flesh
30   Tomorrow, to my bloody creditor.
    Well gaoler, on, pray God Bassanio come
    To see me pay his debt, and then I care not.
                Exeunt.

III. 4

Enter Portia, Nerissa, Lorenzo, Jessica, and a man of Portia's [Balthasar].

LORENZO: Madam, although I speak it in your presence,
   You have a noble and a true conceit 5
   Of god-like amity, which appears most strongly
   In bearing thus the absence of your Lord.
   But if you knew to whom you show this honour,
   How true a Gentleman you send relief,
   How dear a lover of my Lord your husband, 10
   I know you would be prouder of the work
   Than customary bounty can enforce you.
PORTIA: I never did repent for doing good,
   Nor shall not now: for in companions
   That do converse and waste the time together, 15
   Whose souls do bear an egal yoke of love,
   There must be needs a like proportion
   Of lineaments, of manners, and of spirit;
   Which makes me think that this Antonio
   Being the bosom lover of my Lord, 20
   Must needs be like my Lord. If it be so,
   How little is the cost I have bestowed
   In purchasing the semblance of my soul
   From out the state of hellish cruelty;
   This comes too near the praising of myself, 25
   Therefore no more of it: here other things
   Lorenzo I commit into your hands,
   The husbandry and manage of my house,
   Until my Lord's return; for mine own part
   I have toward heaven breath'd a secret vow, 30
   To live in prayer and contemplation,

Only attended by Nerissa here,
Until her husband and my Lord's return:
There is a monastery two miles off,
And there we will abide. I do desire you
5   Not to deny this imposition,
The which my love and some necessity
Now lays upon you.

LORENZO: Madam, with all my heart,
I shall obey you in all fair commands.

10 PORTIA: My people do already know my mind,
And will acknowledge you and Jessica
In place of Lord Bassanio and myself.
So fare you well till we shall meet again.

LORENZO: Fair thoughts and happy hours attend on you.

15 JESSICA: I wish your Ladyship all heart's content.

PORTIA: I thank you for your wish, and am well pleas'd
To wish it back on you: fare you well Jessica.

Exeunt Jessica and Lorenzo.

Now Balthasar, as I have ever found thee honest-true,
20 So let me find thee still: take this same letter,
And use thou all the endeavour of a man,
In speed to Padua, see thou render this
Into my cousin's hand, Doctor Bellario,
And look what notes and garments he doth give thee,
25 Bring them I pray thee with imagin'd speed
Unto the Tranect, to the common ferry
Which trades to Venice; waste no time in words,
But get thee gone, I shall be there before thee.

BALTHASAR: Madam, I go with all convenient speed.

30   *Exit.*

PORTIA: Come on Nerissa, I have work in hand
That you yet know not of; we 'll see our husbands
Before they think of us!

NERISSA: Shall they see us?

PORTIA: They shall Nerissa: but in such a habit,
    That they shall think we are accomplished
    With that we lack; I'll hold thee any wager
    When we are both accoutred like young men,   5
    I'll prove the prettier fellow of the two,
    And wear my dagger with the braver grace,
    And speak between the change of man and boy,
    With a reed voice, and turn two mincing steps
    Into a manly stride; and speak of frays   10
    Like a fine bragging youth: and tell quaint lies
    How honourable Ladies sought my love,
    Which I denying, they fell sick and died.
    I could not do withal: then I'll repent,
    And wish for all that, that I had not kill'd them;   15
    And twenty of these puny lies I'll tell,
    The men shall swear I have discontinued school
    Above a twelvemonth: I have within my mind
    A thousand raw tricks of these bragging Jacks,
    Which I will practise.   20

NERISSA: Why, shall we turn to men?

PORTIA: Fie, what a question's that,
    If thou wert near a lewd interpreter:
    But come, I'll tell thee all my whole device
    When I am in my coach, which stays for us   25
    At the Park gate; and therefore haste away,
    For we must measure twenty miles today.

                Exeunt.

III. 5

Enter Clown and Jessica.

LAUNCELOT: Yes truly; for look you, the sins of the
Father are to be laid upon the children, therefore I pro-
5   mise you, I fear you, I was always plain with you, and so
now I speak my agitation of the matter: therefore be of
good cheer, for truly I think you are damn'd, there is but
one hope in it that can do you any good, and that is but a
kind of bastard hope neither.

10 JESSICA: And what hope is that I pray thee?

LAUNCELOT: Marry you may partly hope that your father
got you not, that you are not the Jew's daughter.

JESSICA: That were a kind of bastard hope indeed, so the
sins of my mother should be visited upon me.

15 LAUNCELOT: Truly then I fear you are damned both by
father and mother: thus when I shun Scylla your father,
I fall into Charybdis your mother; well, you are gone
both ways.

JESSICA: I shall be sav'd by my husband, he hath made me
20 a Christian.

LAUNCELOT: Truly the more to blame he, we were Christians enow before, e'en as many as could well live one by
another: this making of Christians will raise the price of
hogs, if we grow all to be pork-eaters, we shall not shortly
25 have a rasher on the coals for money.

Enter Lorenzo.

JESSICA: I 'll tell my husband Launcelot what you say,
here he comes.

LORENZO: I shall grow jealous of you shortly Launcelot, if
30 you thus get my wife into corners.

JESSICA: Nay, you need not fear us Lorenzo, Launcelot

and I are out, he tells me flatly there is no mercy for me in heaven, because I am a Jew's daughter: and he says you are no good member of the commonwealth, for in converting Jews to Christians, you raise the price of pork.

LORENZO: I shall answer that better to the commonwealth, 5 than you can the getting up of the negro's belly: the Moor is with child by you Launcelot.

LAUNCELOT: It is much that the Moor should be more than reason: but if she be less than an honest woman, she is indeed more than I took her for. 10

LORENZO: How every fool can play upon the word, I think the best grace of wit will shortly turn into silence, and discourse grow commendable in none only but parrots: go in sirrah, bid them prepare for dinner.

LAUNCELOT: That is done sir, they have all stomachs. 15

LORENZO: Goodly Lord, what a wit-snapper are you, then bid them prepare dinner.

LAUNCELOT: That is done too sir, only cover is the word.

LORENZO: Will you cover then sir?

LAUNCELOT: Not so sir neither, I know my duty. 20

LORENZO: Yet more quarrelling with occasion, wilt thou show the whole wealth of thy wit in an instant; I pray thee understand a plain man in his plain meaning: go to thy fellows, bid them cover the table, serve in the meat, and we will come into dinner. 25

LAUNCELOT: For the table sir, it shall be serv'd in, for the meat sir, it shall be covered, for your coming in to dinner sir, why let it be as humours and conceits shall govern.

Exit Clown.

LORENZO: O dear discretion, how his words are suited, 30
The fool hath planted in his memory
An army of good words, and I do know
A many fools that stand in better place,

Garnish'd like him, that for a tricksy word
Defy the matter: how cheer'st thou Jessica,
And now good sweet say thy opinion,
How dost thou like the Lord Bassanio's wife?

5 JESSICA: Past all expressing, it is very meet
The Lord Bassanio live an upright life
For having such a blessing in his Lady,
He finds the joys of heaven here on earth,
And if on earth he do not mean it, it
10 Is reason he should never come to heaven.
Why, if two gods should play some heavenly match,
And on the wager lay two earthly women,
And Portia one: there must be something else
Pawn'd with the other, for the poor rude world
15 Hath not her fellow.

LORENZO: Even such a husband
Hast thou of me, as she is for a wife.

JESSICA: Nay, but ask my opinion too of that.

LORENZO: I will anon, first let us go to dinner.

20 JESSICA: Nay, let me praise you while I have a stomach.

LORENZO: No pray thee, let it serve for table-talk,
Then howsome'er thou speak'st 'mong other things
I shall digest it.

JESSICA: Well, I'll set you forth.

25   *Exeunt.*

IV. 1

Enter the Duke, the Magnificoes, Antonio, Bassanio,
Gratiano, Salerio, and others.

DUKE: What, is Antonio here?

30 ANTONIO: Ready, so please your Grace.

DUKE: I am sorry for thee, thou art come to answer

A stony adversary, an inhuman wretch,
Uncapable of pity, void, and empty
From any dram of mercy.

ANTONIO: I have heard
Your Grace hath ta'en great pains to qualify   5
His rigorous course: but since he stands obdurate,
And that no lawful means can carry me
Out of his envy's reach, I do oppose
My patience to his fury, and am arm'd
To suffer with a quietness of spirit,   10
The very tyranny and rage of his.

DUKE: Go one and call the Jew into the Court.

SALERIO: He is ready at the door, he comes my Lord.

Enter Shylock.

DUKE: Make room, and let him stand before our face. 15
Shylock the world thinks, and I think so too
That thou but leadest this fashion of thy malice
To the last hour of act, and then 'tis thought
Thou 'lt show thy mercy and remorse more strange,
Than is thy strange apparent cruelty;   20
And where thou now exact'st the penalty,
Which is a pound of this poor Merchant's flesh,
Thou wilt not only loose the forfeiture,
But touch'd with human gentleness and love,
Forgive a moiety of the principal,   25
Glancing an eye of pity on his losses
That have of late so huddled on his back,
Enow to press a royal Merchant down,
And pluck commiseration of his state
From brassy bosoms, and rough hearts of flints,   30
From stubborn Turks and Tartars never train'd
To offices of tender courtesy;
We all expect a gentle answer Jew.

SHYLOCK: I have possess'd your Grace of what I purpose,
And by our holy Sabbath have I sworn
To have the due and forfeit of my bond.
If you deny it, let the danger light
5   Upon your Charter, and your City's freedom.
You 'll ask me why I rather choose to have
A weight of carrion flesh, than to receive
Three thousand ducats? I 'll not answer that:
But say it is my humour; Is it answered?
10 What if my house be troubled with a rat,
And I be pleas'd to give ten thousand ducats
To have it ban'd? What, are you answer'd yet?
Some men there are love not a gaping pig:
Some that are mad if they behold a cat:
15 And others, when the bagpipe sings i' th' nose,
Cannot contain their urine for affection.
Masters of passion sways it to the mood
Of what it likes or loathes, now for your answer:
As there is no firm reason to be render'd
20 Why he cannot abide a gaping pig,
Why he a harmless necessary cat,
Why he a woollen bag-pipe: but of force
Must yield to such inevitable shame,
As to offend himself being offended:
25 So can I give no reason, nor I will not,
More than a lodg'd hate, and a certain loathing
I bear Antonio, that I follow thus
A losing suit against him. Are you answered?
BASSANIO: This is no answer thou unfeeling man,
30 To excuse the current of thy cruelty.
SHYLOCK: I am not bound to please thee with my answer.
BASSANIO: Do all men kill the things they do not love?
SHYLOCK: Hates any man the thing he would not kill?

BASSANIO: Every offence is not a hate at first.

SHYLOCK: What wouldst thou have a serpent sting thee twice?

ANTONIO: I pray you think you question with the Jew:
You may as well go stand upon the beach,   5
And bid the main flood bate his usual height,
You may as well use question with the wolf,
Why he hath made the ewe bleat for the lamb:
You may as well forbid the mountain pines
To wag their high tops, and to make no noise   10
When they are fretted with the gusts of heaven:
You may as well do any thing most hard,
As seek to soften that, than which what 's harder:
His Jewish heart. Therefore I do beseech you
Make no more offers, use no farther means,   15
But with all brief and plain conveniency
Let me have judgement, and the Jew his will.

BASSANIO: For thy three thousand ducats here is six.

SHYLOCK: If every ducat in six thousand ducats
Were in six parts, and every part a ducat,   20
I would not draw them, I would have my bond.

DUKE: How shalt thou hope for mercy, rendering none?

SHYLOCK: What judgement shall I dread doing no wrong?
You have among you many a purchas'd slave,
Which like your asses, and your dogs and mules,   25
You use in abject and in slavish parts,
Because you bought them. Shall I say to you,
Let them be free, marry them to your heirs?
Why sweat they under burthens? Let their beds
Be made as soft as yours: and let their palates   30
Be season'd with such viands: you will answer
The slaves are ours. So do I answer you.
The pound of flesh which I demand of him

Is dearly bought, 'tis mine, and I will have it.
If you deny me; fie upon your Law,
There is no force in the decrees of Venice;
I stand for judgement, answer. Shall I have it?

5 DUKE: Upon my power I may dismiss this Court,
Unless Bellario a learned Doctor,
Whom I have sent for to determine this,
Come here today.

SALERIO: My Lord, here stays without

10 A messenger with letters from the Doctor,
New come from Padua.

DUKE: Bring us the letters, call the messenger.

BASSANIO: Good cheer Antonio. What man, courage
yet:

15 The Jew shall have my flesh, blood, bones, and all,
Ere thou shalt lose for me one drop of blood.

ANTONIO: I am a tainted wether of the flock,
Meetest for death, the weakest kind of fruit
Drops earliest to the ground, and so let me;

20 You cannot better be employ'd Bassanio,
Than to live still, and write mine epitaph.

Enter Nerissa [dressed like a lawyer's clerk].

DUKE: Came you from Padua from Bellario?

NERISSA: From both.

25 My Lord Bellario greets your Grace.

BASSANIO: Why dost thou whet thy knife so earnestly?

SHYLOCK: To cut the forfeiture from that bankrout there.

GRATIANO: Not on thy sole: but on thy soul harsh Jew
Thou mak'st thy knife keen: but no metal can,

30 No, not the hangman's axe bear half the keenness
Of thy sharp envy. Can no prayers pierce thee?

SHYLOCK: No, none that thou hast wit enough to make.

GRATIANO: O be thou damn'd, inexecrable dog,

And for thy life let justice be accus'd:
Thou almost mak'st me waver in my faith;
To hold opinion with Pythagoras,
That souls of animals infuse themselves
Into the trunks of men. Thy currish spirit   5
Govern'd a Wolf, who hang'd for human slaughter,
Even from the gallows did his fell soul fleet;
And whilst thou lay'st in thy unhallowed dam,
Infus'd itself in thee: for thy desires
Are wolvish, bloody, starv'd, and ravenous.   10

SHYLOCK: Till thou canst rail the seal from off my bond
Thou but offend'st thy lungs to speak so loud:
Repair thy wit good youth, or it will fall
To endless ruin. I stand here for Law.

DUKE: This letter from Bellario doth commend   15
A young and learned Doctor to our Court;
Where is he?

NERISSA: He attendeth here hard by
To know your answer, whether you 'll admit him.

DUKE: With all my heart. Some three or four of you   20
Go give him courteous conduct to this place,
Meantime the Court shall hear Bellario's letter.

*Your Grace shall understand, that at the receipt of your
letter I am very sick: but in the instant that your messenger
came, in loving visitation, was with me a young Doctor of*   25
*Rome, his name is Balthasar: I acquainted him with the cause
in controversy, between the Jew and Antonio the Merchant:
we turn'd o'er many books together: he is furnished with my
opinion, which better'd with his own learning, the greatness
whereof I cannot enough commend, comes with him at my*   30
*importunity, to fill up your Grace's request in my stead. I be-
seech you, let his lack of years be no impediment to let him lack
a reverend estimation: for I never knew so young a body, with*

so old a head. I leave him to your gracious acceptance, whose
trial shall better publish his commendation.

Enter Portia as Balthasar.

DUKE: You hear the learn'd Bellario what he writes,
5   And here (I take it) is the Doctor come.
     Give me your hand: came you from old Bellario?
PORTIA: I did my Lord.
DUKE: You are welcome: take your place;
     Are you acquainted with the difference
10   That holds this present question in the Court?
PORTIA: I am informed throughly of the cause.
     Which is the Merchant here? and which the Jew?
DUKE: Antonio and old Shylock, both stand forth.
PORTIA: Is your name Shylock?
15 SHYLOCK: Shylock is my name.
PORTIA: Of a strange nature is the suit you follow,
     Yet in such rule, that the Venetian Law
     Cannot impugn you as you do proceed.
     You stand within his danger, do you not?
20 ANTONIO: Ay, so he says.
PORTIA: Do you confess the bond?
ANTONIO: I do.
PORTIA: Then must the Jew be merciful.
SHYLOCK: On what compulsion must I? Tell me that.
25 PORTIA: The quality of mercy is not strain'd,
     It droppeth as the gentle rain from heaven
     Upon the place beneath. It is twice blest,
     It blesseth him that gives, and him that takes,
     'Tis mightiest in the mightiest, it becomes
30   The throned Monarch better than his Crown.
     His Sceptre shows the force of temporal power,
     The attribute to awe and majesty,
     Wherein doth sit the dread and fear of Kings:

But mercy is above this sceptred sway,
It is enthroned in the hearts of Kings,
It is an attribute to God himself;
And earthly power doth then show likest God's
When mercy seasons Justice. Therefore Jew,   5
Though Justice be thy plea, consider this,
That in the course of Justice, none of us
Should see salvation: we do pray for mercy,
And that same prayer, doth teach us all to render
The deeds of mercy. I have spoke thus much   10
To mitigate the justice of thy plea:
Which if thou follow, this strict Court of Venice
Must needs give sentence 'gainst the Merchant there.

SHYLOCK: My deeds upon my head, I crave the Law,
The penalty and forfeit of my bond.   15

PORTIA: Is he not able to discharge the money?

BASSANIO: Yes, here I tender it for him in the Court,
Yea, twice the sum, if that will not suffice,
I will be bound to pay it ten times o'er,
On forfeit of my hands, my head, my heart: 20
If this will not suffice, it must appear
That malice bears down truth. And I beseech you
Wrest once the Law to your authority.
To do a great right, do a little wrong,
And curb this cruel devil of his will.   25

PORTIA: It must not be, there is no power in Venice
Can alter a decree established:
'Twill be recorded for a precedent,
And many an error by the same example,
Will rush into the state: it cannot be.   30

SHYLOCK: A Daniel come to judgement, yea a Daniel.
O wise young Judge, how do I honour thee.

PORTIA: I pray you let me look upon the bond.

i

SHYLOCK: Here' tis most reverend Doctor, here it is.

PORTIA: Shylock, there's thrice thy money offered thee.

SHYLOCK: An oath, an oath, I have an oath in heaven:
    Shall I lay perjury upon my soul?
5   No not for Venice.

PORTIA: Why this bond is forfeit,
    And lawfully by this the Jew may claim
    A pound of flesh, to be by him cut off
    Nearest the Merchant's heart; be merciful,
10   Take thrice thy money, bid me tear the bond.

SHYLOCK: When it is paid according to the tenour.
    It doth appear you are a worthy Judge:
    You know the Law, your exposition
    Hath been most sound. I charge you by the Law,
15   Whereof you are a well-deserving pillar,
    Proceed to judgement: By my soul I swear,
    There is no power in the tongue of man
    To alter me: I stay here on my bond.

ANTONIO: Most heartily I do beseech the Court
20   To give the judgement.

PORTIA: Why then thus it is:
    You must prepare your bosom for his knife.

SHYLOCK: O noble Judge, O excellent young man.

PORTIA: For the intent and purpose of the Law
25   Hath full relation to the penalty,
    Which here appeareth due upon the bond.

SHYLOCK: 'Tis very true: O wise and upright Judge,
    How much more elder art thou than thy looks.

PORTIA: Therefore lay bare your bosom.

30 SHYLOCK: Ay, his breast,
    So says the bond, doth it not noble Judge?
    Nearest his heart, those are the very words.

PORTIA: It is so: Are there balance here to weigh

  The flesh?

SHYLOCK: I have them ready.

PORTIA: Have by some surgeon Shylock on your charge
  To stop his wounds, lest he should bleed to death.

SHYLOCK: Is it so nominated in the bond?   5

PORTIA: It is not so express'd: but what of that?
  'Twere good you do so much for charity.

SHYLOCK: I cannot find it, 'tis not in the bond.

PORTIA: You Merchant, have you any thing to say?

ANTONIO: But little: I am arm'd and well prepar'd.   10
  Give me your hand Bassanio, fare you well,
  Grieve not that I am fallen to this for you:
  For herein Fortune shows herself more kind
  Than is her custom. It is still her use
  To let the wretched man outlive his wealth,   15
  To view with hollow eye, and wrinkled brow
  An age of poverty. From which lingering penance
  Of such misery, doth she cut me off:
  Commend me to your honourable wife,
  Tell her the process of Antonio's end: 20
  Say how I lov'd you; speak me fair in death:
  And when the tale is told, bid her be judge,
  Whether Bassanio had not once a Love:
  Repent not you that you shall lose your friend,
  And he repents not that he pays your debt.   25
  For if the Jew do cut but deep enough,
  I'll pay it instantly, with all my heart.

BASSANIO: Antonio, I am married to a wife,
  Which is as dear to me as life itself,
  But life itself, my wife, and all the world,   30
  Are not with me esteem'd above thy life.
  I would lose all, ay sacrifice them all
  Here to this devil, to deliver you.

PORTIA: Your wife would give you little thanks for that
    If she were by to hear you make the offer.
GRATIANO: I have a wife whom I protest I love,
    I would she were in heaven, so she could
5   Entreat some power to change this currish Jew.
NERISSA: 'Tis well you offer it behind her back,
    The wish would make else an unquiet house.
SHYLOCK: These be the Christian husbands: I have a
    daughter,
10   Would any of the stock of Barrabas
    Had been her husband, rather than a Christian.
    We trifle time, I pray thee pursue sentence.
PORTIA: A pound of that same Merchant's flesh is thine,
    The Court awards it, and the Law doth give it.
15 SHYLOCK: Most rightful Judge.
PORTIA: And you must cut this flesh from off his breast,
    The Law allows it, and the Court awards it.
SHYLOCK: Most learned Judge, a sentence, come prepare.
PORTIA: Tarry a little, there is something else,
20   This bond doth give thee here no jot of blood,
    The words expressly are a pound of flesh:
    Then take thy bond, take thou thy pound of flesh,
    But in the cutting it, if thou dost shed.
    One drop of Christian blood, thy lands and goods
25   Are by the Laws of Venice confiscate
    Unto the State of Venice.
GRATIANO: O upright Judge,
    Mark Jew, O learned Judge.
SHYLOCK: Is that the Law?
30 PORTIA: Thyself shalt see the Act:
    For as thou urgest justice, be assur'd
    Thou shalt have justice more than thou desirest.
GRATIANO: O learned Judge, mark Jew, a learned Judge.

SHYLOCK: I take this offer then, pay the bond thrice,
   And let the Christian go.
BASSANIO: Here is the money.
PORTIA: Soft, the Jew shall have all justice, soft, no haste,
   He shall have nothing but the penalty.   5
GRATIANO: O Jew, an upright Judge, a learned Judge.
PORTIA: Therefore prepare thee to cut off the flesh,
   Shed thou no blood, nor cut thou less nor more
   But just a pound of flesh: if thou tak'st more
   Or less than a just pound, be it but so much   10
   As makes it light or heavy in the substance,
   Or the division of the twentieth part
   Of one poor scruple, nay if the scale do turn
   But in the estimation of a hair,
   Thou diest, and all thy goods are confiscate.   15
GRATIANO: A second Daniel, a Daniel Jew,
   Now infidel I have thee on the hip.
PORTIA: Why doth the Jew pause, take thy forfeiture.
SHYLOCK: Give me my principal, and let me go.
BASSANIO: I have it ready for thee, here it is.   20
PORTIA: He hath refus'd it in the open Court,
   He shall have merely justice and his bond.
GRATIANO: A Daniel still say I, a second Daniel,
   I thank thee Jew for teaching me that word.
SHYLOCK: Shall I not have barely my principal?   25
PORTIA: Thou shalt have nothing but the forfeiture,
   To be so taken at thy peril Jew.
SHYLOCK: Why then the Devil give him good of it:
   I'll stay no longer question.
PORTIA: Tarry Jew,   30
   The Law hath yet another hold on you.
   It is enacted in the Laws of Venice,
   If it be prov'd against an Alien,

That by direct, or indirect attempts
Hc seek the life of any Citizen,
The party 'gainst the which he doth contrive,
Shall seize one half his goods, the other half
5   Comes to the privy coffer of the State,
And the offender's life lies in the mercy
Of the Duke only, 'gainst all other voice.
In which predicament I say thou stand'st:
For it appears by manifest proceeding,
10   That indirectly, and directly too,
Thou hast contriv'd against the very life
Of the defendant: and thou hast incurr'd
The danger formerly by me rehears'd.
Down therefore, and beg mercy of the Duke.

15 GRATIANO: Beg that thou mayst have leave to hang thy-
    self,
And yet thy wealth being forfeit to the State,
Thou hast not left the value of a cord,
Therefore thou must be hang'd at the State's charge.

20 DUKE: That thou shalt see the difference of our spirit,
I pardon thee thy life before thou ask it:
For half thy wealth, it is Antonio's,
The other half comes to the general State,
Which humbleness may drive unto a fine.

25 PORTIA: Ay for the State, not for Antonio.

SHYLOCK: Nay, take my life and all, pardon not that,
You take my house, when you do take the prop
That doth sustain my house: you take my life
When you do take the means whereby I live.

30 PORTIA: What mercy can you render him Antonio?

GRATIANO: A halter *gratis*, nothing else for God's sake.

ANTONIO: So please my Lord the Duke, and all the Court
To quit the fine for one half of his goods,

I am content: so he will let me have
The other half in use, to render it
Upon his death, unto the Gentleman
That lately stole his daughter.
Two things provided more, that for this favour   5
He presently become a Christian:
The other, that he do record a gift
Here in the Court of all he dies possess'd
Unto his son Lorenzo, and his daughter.

DUKE: He shall do this, or else I do recant   10
The pardon that I late pronounced here.

PORTIA: Art thou contented Jew? what dost thou say?

SHYLOCK: I am content.

PORTIA: Clerk, draw a deed of gift.

SHYLOCK: I pray you give me leave to go from hence,   15
I am not well, send the deed after me,
And I will sign it.

DUKE: Get thee gone, but do it.

GRATIANO: In christening thou shalt have two godfathers,
Had I been Judge, thou shouldst have had ten more,   20
To bring thee to the gallows, not to the font.

Exit Shylock.

DUKE: Sir I entreat you with me home to dinner.

PORTIA: I humbly do desire your Grace of pardon,
I must away this night toward Padua,   25
And it is meet I presently set forth.

DUKE: I am sorry that your leisure serves you not:
Antonio, gratify this gentleman,
For in my mind you are much bound to him.

Exit Duke and his train.   30

BASSANIO: Most wort gentleman, I and my friend
Have by your wisdom been this day acquitted
Of grievous penalties, in lieu whereof,

Three thousand ducats due unto the Jew
We freely cope your courteous pains withal.

ANTONIO: And stand indebted over and above
In love and service to you evermore.

5 PORTIA: He is well paid that is well satisfied,
And I delivering you, am satisfied,
And therein do account myself well paid,
My mind was never yet more mercenary.
I pray you know me when we meet again,
10 I wish you well, and so I take my leave.

BASSANIO: Dear sir, of force I must attempt you further,
Take some remembrance of us as a tribute,
Not as a fee: grant me two things, I pray you
Not to deny me, and to pardon me.

15 PORTIA: You press me far, and therefore I will yield,
Give me your gloves, I 'll wear them for your sake,
And for your love I 'll take this ring from you,
Do not draw back your hand, I 'll take no more,
And you in love shall not deny me this.

20 BASSANIO: This ring good sir, alas it is a trifle,
I will not shame myself to give you this.

PORTIA: I will have nothing else but only this,
And now methinks I have a mind to it.

BASSANIO: There's more depends on this than on the value,
25 The dearest ring in Venice will I give you,
And find it out by proclamation,
Only for this I pray you pardon me.

PORTIA: I see sir you are liberal in offers,
You taught me first to beg, and now methinks
30 You teach me how a beggar should be answer'd.

BASSANIO: Good sir, this ring was given me by my wife,
And when she put it on, she made me vow
That I should neither sell, nor give, nor lose it.

PORTIA: That 'scuse serves many men to save their gifts,
    And if your wife be not a mad woman,
    And know how well I have deserv'd this ring,
    She would not hold out enemy for ever
    For giving it to me: well, peace be with you.   5
            Exeunt Portia and Nerissa.
ANTONIO: My Lord Bassanio, let him have the ring,
    Let his deservings and my love withal
    Be valued gainst your wife's commandment.
BASSANIO: Go Gratiano, run and overtake him,   10
    Give him the ring, and bring him if thou canst
    Unto Antonio's house, away, make haste.
            Exit Gratiano.
    Come, you and I will thither presently,
    And in the morning early will we both   15
    Fly toward Belmont, come Antonio.
            Exeunt.

IV.2

Enter Portia and Nerissa.

PORTIA: Inquire the Jew's house out, give him this deed,   20
    And let him sign it, we 'll away tonight,
    And be a day before our husbands home:
    This deed will be well welcome to Lorenzo.
            Enter Gratiano.
GRATIANO: Fair sir, you are well o'erta'en: 25
    My Lord Bassanio upon more advice,
    Hath sent you here this ring, and doth entreat
    Your company at dinner.
PORTIA: That cannot be;
    His ring I do accept most thankfully,   30
    And so I pray you tell him: furthermore,

I pray you show my youth old Shylock's house.

GRATIANO: That will I do.

NERISSA: Sir, I would speak with you:

I 'll see if I can get my husband's ring

5   Which I did make him swear to keep for ever.

PORTIA: Thou mayst I warrant, we shall have old swear-
    ing

That they did give the rings away to men;

But we 'll out-face them, and out-swear them too:

10   Away, make haste, thou know'st where I will tarry.

NERISSA: Come good sir, will you show me to this house.

Exeunt.

V. I

Enter Lorenzo and Jessica.

15 LORENZO: The moon shines bright. In such a night as this,
    When the sweet wind did gently kiss the trees,
    And they did make no noise, in such a night
    Troylus methinks mounted the Trojan walls,
    And sigh'd his soul towards the Grecian tents

20   Where Cressid lay that night.

JESSICA: In such a night
    Did Thisbe fearfully o'er-trip the dew,
    And saw the lion's shadow ere himself,
    And ran dismayed away.

25 LORENZO: In such a night
    Stood Dido with a willow in her hand
    Upon the wild sea banks, and waft her love
    To come again to Carthage.

JESSICA: In such a night

30   Medea gather'd the enchanted herbs
    That did renew old Aeson.

LORENZO: In such a night
  Did Jessica steal from the wealthy Jew,
  And with an unthrift Love did run from Venice,
  As far as Belmont.

JESSICA: In such a night   5
  Did young Lorenzo swear he lov'd her well,
  Stealing her soul with many vows of faith,
  And ne'er a true one.

LORENZO: In such a night
  Did pretty Jessica (like a little shrew)   10
  Slander her love, and he forgave it her.

JESSICA: I would out-night you did no body come:
  But hark, I hear the footing of a man.

Enter Messenger.

LORENZO: Who comes so fast in silence of the night?   15

MESSENGER: A friend.

LORENZO: A friend, what friend? your name I pray you
  friend?

MESSENGER: Stephano is my name, and I bring word
  My Mistress will before the break of day   20
  Be here at Belmont, she doth stray about
  By holy crosses where she kneels and prays
  For happy wedlock hours.

LORENZO: Who comes with her?

MESSENGER: None but a holy Hermit and her maid: 25
  I pray you is my Master yet return'd?

LORENZO: He is not, nor we have not heard from him,
  But go we in I pray thee Jessica,
  And ceremoniously let us prepare
  Some welcome for the Mistress of the house.   30

Enter Clown.

LAUNCELOT: Sola, sola: wo ha ho, sola, sola.

LORENZO: Who calls?

LAUNCELOT: Sola, did you see Master Lorenzo? Master
    Lorenzo, sola, sola.
LORENZO: Leave hollowing man, here.
LAUNCELOT: Sola, where, where?
5 LORENZO: Here!
LAUNCELOT: Tell him there's a post come from my
    Master, with his horn full of good news, my Master will
    be here ere morning.

                         Exit.

10 LORENZO: Sweet soul let's in, and there expect their com-
        ing.
    And yet no matter: why should we go in?
    My friend Stephano, signify I pray you
    Within the house, your Mistress is at hand,
15 And bring your music forth into the air.

                         Exit.

    How sweet the moonlight sleeps upon this bank,
    Here will we sit, and let the sounds of music
    Creep in our ears; soft stillness, and the night
20 Become the touches of sweet harmony:
    Sit Jessica, look how the floor of heaven
    Is thick inlaid with patens of bright gold,
    There's not the smallest orb which thou behold'st
    But in his motion like an angel sings,
25 Still quiring to the young-eyed cherubins;
    Such harmony is in immortal souls,
    But whilst this muddy vesture of decay
    Doth grossly close it in, we cannot hear it:
    Come ho, and wake Diana with a hymn,
30 With sweetest touches pierce your Mistress' ear,
    And draw her home with music.
JESSICA: I am never merry when I hear sweet music.
                         Play Music.

LORENZO: The reason is, your spirits are attentive:
  For do but note a wild and wanton herd
  Or race of youthful and unhandled colts,
  Fetching mad bounds, bellowing and neighing loud,
  Which is the hot condition of their blood,   5
  If they but hear perchance a trumpet sound,
  Or any air of music touch their ears,
  You shall perceive them make a mutual stand,
  Their savage eyes turn'd to a modest gaze,
  By the sweet power of music: therefore the Poet   10
  Did feign that Orpheus drew trees, stones, and floods,
  Since nought so stockish, hard, and full of rage,
  But music for the time doth change his nature.
  The man that hath no music in himself,
  Nor is not moved with concord of sweet sounds,   15
  Is fit for treasons, stratagems, and spoils,
  The motions of his spirit are dull as night,
  And his affections dark as Erebus,
  Let no such man be trusted: mark the music.

          Enter Portia and Nerissa.   20

PORTIA: That light we see is burning in my hall:
  How far that little candle throws his beams,
  So shines a good deed in a naughty world.

NERISSA: When the moon shone we did not see the candle.

PORTIA: So doth the greater glory dim the less,   25
  A substitute shines brightly as a King
  Until a King be by, and then his state
  Empties itself, as doth an inland brook
  Into the main of waters: music, hark.

          Music.   30

NERISSA: It is your music Madam of the house.

PORTIA: Nothing is good I see without respect,
  Methinks it sounds much sweeter than by day.

NERISSA: Silence bestows that virtue on it Madam.

PORTIA: The crow doth sing as sweetly as the lark
When neither is attended: and I think
The nightingale if she should sing by day
5 When every goose is cackling, would be thought
No better a musician than the wren.
How many things by season, season'd are
To their right praise, and true perfection:
Peace, now the Moon sleeps with Endymion,
10 And would not be awak'd.

Music ceases.

LORENZO: That is the voice,
Or I am much deceiv'd of Portia.

PORTIA: He knows me as the blind man knows the cuckoo
15 by the bad voice.

LORENZO: Dear Lady welcome home.

PORTIA: We have been praying for our husbands' welfare
Which speed we hope the better for our words:
Are they return'd?

20 LORENZO: Madam, they are not yet:
But there is come a messenger before
To signify their coming.

PORTIA: Go in Nerissa,
Give order to my servants, that they take
25 No note at all of our being absent hence,
Nor you Lorenzo, Jessica nor you.

A tucket sounds.

LORENZO: Your husband is at hand, I hear his trumpet,
We are no tell-tales Madam, fear you not.

30 PORTIA: This night methinks is but the daylight sick,
It looks a little paler, 'tis a day,
Such as the day is, when the Sun is hid.

Enter Bassanio, Antonio, Gratiano, and their followers.

BASSANIO: We should hold day with the Antipodes,
If you would walk in absence of the sun.

PORTIA: Let me give light, but let me not be light,
For a light wife doth make a heavy husband,
And never be Bassanio so for me,   5
But God sort all: you are welcome home my Lord.

BASSANIO: I thank you Madam, give welcome to my
friend;
This is the man, this is Antonio,
To whom I am so infinitely bound.   10

PORTIA: You should in all sense be much bound to him,
For as I hear he was much bound for you.

ANTONIO: No more than I am well acquainted of.

PORTIA: Sir, you are very welcome to our house:
It must appear in other ways than words,   15
Therefore I scant this breathing courtesy.

GRATIANO: By yonder Moon I swear you do me wrong,
In faith I gave it to the Judge's Clerk,
Would he were gelt that had it for my part,
Since you do take it Love so much at heart.   20

PORTIA: A quarrel ho already, what's the matter?

GRATIANO: About a hoop of gold, a paltry ring
That she did give me, whose posy was
For all the world like cutler's poetry
Upon a knife; *Love me, and leave me not.*   25

NERISSA: What talk you of the posy or the value:
You swore to me when I did give it you,
That you would wear it till the hour of death,
And that it should lie with you in your grave,
Though not for me, yet for your vehement oaths,   30
You should have been respective and have kept it.
Gave it a Judge's Clerk: no, God's my judge
The Clerk will ne'er wear hair on 's face that had it.

GRATIANO: He will, and if he live to be a man.

NERISSA: Ay, if a woman live to be a man.

GRATIANO: Now by this hand I gave it to a youth,
A kind of boy, a little scrubbed boy,
5   No higher than thyself, the Judge's Clerk,
A prating boy that begg'd it as a fee,
I could not for my heart deny it him.

PORTIA: You were to blame, I must be plain with you,
To part so slightly with your wife's first gift,
10   A thing stuck on with oaths upon your finger,
And so riveted with faith unto your flesh.
I gave my Love a ring, and made him swear
Never to part with it, and here he stands:
I dare be sworn for him, he would not leave it,
15   Nor pluck it from his finger, for the wealth
That the world masters. Now in faith Gratiano,
You give your wife too unkind a cause of grief,
And 'twere to me I should be mad at it.

BASSANIO: Why I were best to cut my left hand off,
20   And swear I lost the ring defending it.

GRATIANO: My Lord Bassanio gave his ring away
Unto the Judge that begg'd it, and indeed
Deserv'd it too: and then the boy his Clerk
That took some pains in writing, he begg'd mine,
25   And neither man nor master would take aught
But the two rings.

PORTIA: What ring gave you my Lord?
Not that I hope which you receiv'd of me.

BASSANIO: If I could add a lie unto a fault,
30   I would deny it: but you see my finger
Hath not the ring upon it, it is gone.

PORTIA: Even so void is your false heart of truth.
By heaven I will ne'er come in your bed

Until I see the ring.

NERISSA: Nor I in yours, till I again see mine.

BASSANIO: Sweet Portia,
If you did know to whom I gave the ring,
If you did know for whom I gave the ring,   5
And would conceive for what I gave the ring,
And how unwillingly I left the ring,
When nought would be accepted but the ring,
You would abate the strength of your displeasure.

PORTIA: If you had known the virtue of the ring,   10
Or half her worthiness that gave the ring,
Or your own honour to contain the ring,
You would not then have parted with the ring:
What man is there so much unreasonable,
If you had pleas'd to have defended it   15
With any terms of zeal: wanted the modesty
To urge the thing held as a ceremony:
Nerissa teaches me what to believe,
I'll die for 't, but some woman had the ring.

BASSANIO: No by mine honour Madam, by my soul   20
No woman had it, but a civil Doctor,
Which did refuse three thousand ducats of me,
And begg'd the ring; the which I did deny him,
And suffer'd him to go displeas'd away:
Even he that had held up the very life   25
Of my dear friend. What should I say sweet Lady?
I was enforc'd to send it after him,
I was beset with shame and courtesy,
My honour would not let ingratitude
So much besmear it. Pardon me good Lady,   30
And by these blessed candles of the night,
Had you been there, I think you would have begg'd
The ring of me, to give the worthy Doctor.

PORTIA: Let not that Doctor e'er come near my house,
  Since he hath got the jewel that I loved,
  And that which you did swear to keep for me,
  I will become as liberal as you,
5 I 'll not deny him any thing I have,
  No, not my body, nor my husband's bed:
  Know him I shall, I am well sure of it.
  Lie not a night from home. Watch me like Argos,
  If you do not, if I be left alone,
10 Now by mine honour which is yet mine own,
  I 'll have the Doctor for my bedfellow.

NERISSA: And I his Clerk: therefore be well advis'd
  How you do leave me to mine own protection.

GRATIANO: Well, do you so: let not me take him then,
15 For if I do, I 'll mar the young Clerk's pen.

ANTONIO: I am th' unhappy subject of these quarrels.

PORTIA: Sir, grieve not you, you are welcome notwithstanding.

BASSANIO: Portia, forgive me this enforced wrong,
20 And in the hearing of these many friends
  I swear to thee, even by thine own fair eyes
  Wherein I see myself.

PORTIA: Mark you but that?
  In both my eyes he doubly sees himself:
25 In each eye one, swear by your double self,
  And there 's an oath of credit.

BASSANIO: Nay, but hear me.
  Pardon this fault, and by my soul I swear
  I never more will break an oath with thee.

30 ANTONIO: I once did lend my body for his wealth,
  Which but for him that had your husband's ring
  Had quite miscarried. I dare be bound again,
  My soul upon the forfeit, that your Lord

Will never more break faith advisedly.

PORTIA: Then you shall be his surety: give him this,
   And bid him keep it better than the other.

ANTONIO: Here Lord Bassanio, swear to keep this ring.

BASSANIO: By heaven it is the same I gave the Doctor.   5

PORTIA: I had it of him: pardon me Bassanio,
   For by this ring the Doctor lay with me.

NERISSA: And pardon me my gentle Gratiano,
   For that same scrubbed boy the Doctor's Clerk
   In lieu of this, last night did lie with me.   10

GRATIANO: Why this is like the mending of highways
   In summer, where the ways are fair enough:
   What, are we cuckolds ere we have deserv'd it.

PORTIA: Speak not so grossly, you are all amaz'd;
   Here is a letter, read it at your leisure,   15
   It comes from Padua from Bellario,
   There you shall find that Portia was the Doctor,
   Nerissa there her Clerk. Lorenzo here
   Shall witness I set forth as soon as you,
   And but e'en now return'd: I have not yet   20
   Enter'd my house. Antonio you are welcome,
   And I have better news in store for you
   Than you expect: unseal this letter soon,
   There you shall find three of your Argosie:
   Are richly come to harbour suddenly.   25
   You shall not know by what strange accident
   I chanced on this letter.

ANTONIO: I am dumb.

BASSANIO: Were you the Doctor, and I knew you not?

GRATIANO: Were you the Clerk that is to make me cuck-   30
   old?

NERISSA: Ay, but the Clerk that never means to do it,
   Unless he live until he be a man.

BASSANIO: (Sweet Doctor) you shall be my bedfellow,
When I am absent, then lie with my wife.

ANTONIO: (Sweet Lady) you have given me life and living;
For here I read for certain that my ships

5   Are safely come to road.

PORTIA: How now Lorenzo?
My Clerk hath some good comforts too for you.

NERISSA: Ay, and I 'll give them him without a fee.
There do I give to you and Jessica

10   From the rich Jew, a special deed of gift
After his death, of all he dies possess'd of.

LORENZO: Fair Ladies you drop manna in the way
Of starved people.

PORTIA: It is almost morning,

15   And yet I am sure you are not satisfied
Of these events at full. Let us go in,
And charge us there upon intergatories,
And we will answer all things faithfully.

GRATIANO: Let it be so, the first intergatory

20   That my Nerissa shall be sworn on, is
Whether till the next night she had rather stay
Or go to bed, now being two hours to day:
But were the day come, I should wish it dark,
'Till I were couching with the Doctor's Clerk.

25   Well, while I live, I 'll fear no other thing
So sore, as keeping safe Nerissa's ring.

                    Exeunt.

NOTES

References are to the page and line of this edition;
the full page contains 33 lines.

THE ACTORS' NAMES: *Solanio: Salarino: Salerio:* P. 22
There is some confusion in the original texts about
the names of these unimportant gentlemen. Solanio
is sometimes called Salanio; but I have kept the form
Solanio to lessen the confusion. Neither Solanio nor
Salarino is mentioned in the dialogue. Salerio does
not appear till Act III Scene 2, where he is called 'my
old Venetian friend, Salerio'. One would have ex-
pected Solanio or Salarino, who have appeared
several times before. Perhaps Salerio (as suggested by
Dover Wilson) was identical with Salarino, who
owes his separate existence to a copyist's error. By
way of variant, Salarino is also 'Slarino' and 'Salino'!
Confusions were likely to arise when all three characters were abbreviated to *Sal:* or *Sol:* in the manu-
script.

In sooth . . . so sad: This is the first play in which P. 23 L. 3
Shakespeare opens with the expression of a mood. It
is one indication of the development of his skill as a
dramatist: he was now beginning to gain in subtlety.
Hitherto he had been content with the direct state-
ment of his plot.

portly: swollen, like some prosperous and stout mer- P. 23 L. 10
chant.

pageants: like a show piece in a procession. P. 23 L. 12

over-peer the petty traffickers: look down on little trad- P. 23 L. 13
ing ships.

Andrew: It is possible that Shakespeare used this name P. 23 L. 29
as typical of a great ship because of the great galleon
Saint Andrew which was captured and brought home
in June, 1596, after the sack of Cadiz by the Earl of
Essex and Lord Charles Howard.

P. 23 L. 29   *dock'd*: the original texts read 'docks'.

P. 24 L. 22   *Janus*: a two-headed Roman god.

P. 24 L. 28   *Nestor ... laughable*: Nestor was the old veteran amongst the Greek commanders at Troy, and so the pattern of venerable gravity and experience. If he guaranteed a joke, it must be good.

P. 25 L. 8   *exceeding strange*: very unfriendly.

P. 25 L. 26   *mortifying groans*: sighs were supposed to consume the heart's blood, and so to be deadly.

P. 25 L. 28   *Sit ... grandsire*: sit still and solemn, like a figure on a tomb.

P. 25 L. 33   *cream and mantle*: become covered with a thick motionless scum.

P. 26 L. 2   *with purpose ... opinion*: in order to get a reputation for.

P. 26 L. 11   *I'll tell thee more*: Antonio's glum silence is too much for the talkative Gratiano, who subsides abruptly.

P. 26 L. 12   *melancholy bait*: bait which causes melancholy, for 'opinion' (i.e., reputation) is not worth having.

P. 26 L. 21   *for this gear*: for this matter. 'Gear' is one of those words used loosely for anything – like 'lot' or 'case'.

P. 26 L. 24   *not vendible*: not saleable; whom no one wants.

P. 27 LL. 3–5   *How much ... continuance*: 'how much I have ruined myself by living extravagantly beyond my means.'

P. 27 L. 12   *love ... warranty*: such is your love that I have leave.

P. 27 L. 33–
P. 28 L. 1   *spend ... circumstance*: 'you waste your time by not coming to the point at once.'

P. 28 L. 3   *question ... uttermost*: doubting whether I shall help you to the uttermost of my power.

P. 28
LL. 18–19   *Colchos' ... Jasons*: In Colchos lay the Golden Fleece which Jason fetched away in his ship the *Argo*.

P. 28 L. 25   *commodity*: goods which serve as security for a debt.

P. 29
LL. 9–11   *superfluity ... longer*: a man who has too much wealth grows old quicker than one with modest means.

P. 29 L. 25   *will ... will*: with a pun on Portia's inclination and her father's testament, which bound her to choose her husband by the test of the caskets.

level . . . affection: guess how I like them. *Level*: aim   P. 30 L. 7
at, guess. These descriptions of national characteristics
were popular. Nashe, for instance, in *Piers Penniless*
(1591), one of the most popular of Elizabethan books,
gives a long catalogue of the failings of the various
nations.

death's head . . . : a bare skull, a *memento mori,* the em-   P. 30
blem that we must all die.   LL. 18–19

he understands not me: it has always been a criticism of   P. 31 LL. 1–2
the Englishman that he learns no language but his
own.

proper man's picture: because he looks well but cannot   P. 31 L. 5
talk. *Proper*: handsome.

dumb-show: In some Elizabethan plays the action that   P. 31 L. 6
was to follow was first silently mimed, as in the play
in *Hamlet* (III. 2).

doublet . . . behaviour everywhere: It was a common   P. 31 LL. 7–8
jibe at the travelled Englishman that he adopted the
fashions of all countries at once. *Doublet*: jacket;
Round hose: baggy breeches.   P. 31 L. 7

Scottish Lord: so the Quarto. The Folio tactfully al-   P. 31 L. 9
tered it to 'Other Lord', because after the accession of
James of Scotland to the English throne jibes about
the Scots were no longer seasonable, or safe. When
the play was first written, there was constant ill-feel-
ing between the English and the Scots.

Frenchman . . . surety: In the early years of Queen   P. 31 L. 14
Elizabeth's reign the alliance between the French and
Scots was close. Mary Queen of Scots was herself the
widow of the French Dauphin. *Seal'd under*: agreed
to be his surety.

Sibylla: the ancient prophetess to whom Apollo   P. 32 L. 4
promised that her years should be as many as the
grains of sand which she held in her hand.

complexion of a devil: The Devil was painted as black.   P. 32 L. 29

be bound: shall be guarantor for repayment.   P. 33 L. 7

means . . . supposition: his property is speculative, de-   P. 33 L..19
pending on ventures which have not yet matured.

Rialto: 'The Rialto which is at the farther side of the   P. 33 L. 21

bridge as you come from St Mark's, is a most stately
building, being the Exchange of Venice, where the
Venetian Gentlemen and the Merchants do meet
twice a day, betwixt eleven and twelve of the clock
in the morning, and betwixt five and six of the clock
in the afternoon. This Rialto is of a goodly height,
built all with brick as the Palaces are, adorned with
many fair walks or open galleries that I have before
mentioned, and hath a pretty quadrangular court ad-
joining to it.' – [Coryat's *Crudities*, 1611, Maclehose
edn., i, 312.]

P 34 L. 3   *conjured the devil into:* i.e., the destruction of the
                Gadarene swine (Mark 5: 1–17).

P 34 L. 10   *fawning publican:* In the mouth of a strict Jew 'publi-
                can' is a term of abuse; as in the Parable of the
                Pharisee and the Publican: 'The Pharisee stood and
                prayed thus with himself, God, I thank thee, that I
                am not as other men are, extortioners, unjust, adul-
                terers, or even as this publican'. (Luke 18: 11).

P. 35 L. 8   *Upon advantage:* with interest.

P 35   *This Jacob . . . third:* i.e., Jacob was the grandson of
LL. 11–13   Abraham and, though the younger son of Isaac, in-
                herited the birthright, because his mother by a trick
                caused him to deceive Isaac and so obtain the blessing
                intended for Esau (Genesis 27).

P. 35   *When Laban and himself . . . :* The story is told in
LL. 17–27   Genesis 30: 27–43. Jacob agreed to serve Laban for
                a further period, his hire being the speckled and spot-
                ted cattle and goats, and the brown sheep, 'And
                Jacob took him rods of green poplar, and of the hazel
                and chestnut tree; and pilled white strakes in them
                and made the white appear which was in the rods.
                And he set the rods which he had pilled before the
                flocks in the gutters in the watering troughs when the
                flocks came to drink, that they should conceive when
                they came to drink. And the flocks conceived before
                the rods, and brought forth cattle ringstraked,
                speckled, and spotted. And Jacob did separate the
                lambs, and set the faces of the flocks toward the ring-
                straked, and all the brown in the flock of Laban; and

he put his own flocks by themselves, and put them
not unto Laban's cattle. And it came to pass, whenso-
ever the stronger cattle did conceive, that Jacob laid
the rods before the eyes of the cattle in the gutters,
that they might conceive among the rods'. *streak'd
and pied:* 'ringstraked and spotted'; *rank:* on heat;
pill'd: peeled; *fulsome:* fat; *eaning time:* lambing season; *fall:* let fall.

void your rheum: spit.   P. 36 L. 24

bondman's key: the whining note of a slave.   P. 36 L. 30

single bond: single agreement, made with one person   P. 37 L. 20
alone, without securities.

shadowed livery: i.e., my black skin, which Morocco   P. 39 L. 1
hyperbolically says is a sign that he serves the Sun
(Phoebus).

make incision: cut for bleeding – a surgical term.   P. 39 L. 5

Lichas: the page who brought Hercules (Alcides) the   P. 39 L. 32
poisoned robe that caused his death.

Gobbo: In the First Quarto and Folio the name is spelt   P. 40 L. 22
'Jobbe': in all other editions it is altered to Gobbo.

smack ... taste: 'for my father was not too honest,   P. 41 L. 3
there was a kind of burnt taste about him.' *Smack:*
taste; *grow to:* a phrase used of milk burnt in the pan.

God ... mark: one of those meaningless phrases used   P. 41 L. 8
as an apology for an unpleasant remark.

saving your reverence: 'with apologies' – used as   P. 41 L. 10
introduction to a coarse remark like 'God save the
mark'.

sand blind: nearly blind. Launcelot takes *sand blind*   P. 41 L. 20
to mean 'as if blinded by sand', but his father has
not only sand but gravel in his eyes, for he is com-
pletely sightless.

Talk of young Master Launcelot: Launcelot in fooling   P. 41 L. 31
his old father pretends that he has gone up in the
world and is now an employer not a servant.

well to live: 'poor but honest'.   P. 42 L. 3

hovel-post: the post supporting a hovel.   P. 42 L. 17

set up my rest: determined to stake all – a metaphor   P. 43 L. 19
from the card game of primero.

P. 43
LL. 26-7   *I am a Jew:* a common term of reproach, 'I am a villain'.

P. 44 L. 3   *Gramercy:* God have mercy – an expression of thanks.

P. 44 L. 7   *infection:* Like other humble characters in Shakespeare's plays, the Gobbos like to use long words but do not always choose the right one. *Infection:* affection; *defect:* effect; *frutify:* certify.

P. 44 L. 30   *the old proverb:* i.e., 'the Grace of God is better than riches'.

P. 45 LL. 5-6   *if . . . fairer table:* Here Launcelot practises a little palmistry on his own hand to prophesy a good and interesting fortune for himself. *Table:* palm of the hand.

P. 46 L. 10   *with respect:* like a sober and respectable person.

P. 46 L. 14   *observance of civility:* observe polite behaviour.

P. 47 L. 8   *exhibit my tongue:* show what I would like to say; or else, *exhibit:* prohibit, prevent me from speaking.

P. 47 L. 25   *Disguise us:* don our masks.

P. 47 L. 28   *Quaintly ordered:* ingeniously carried out.

P. 48 L. 15   *Masque:* a form of evening entertainment, particularly in Italy, to which the guests went masked. Shakespeare introduces another masque in *Romeo and Juliet* (I. 4).

P. 50 LL. 1-2   *Black Monday:* Easter Monday, 1360, so called because it was so cold that many of the English then besieging Paris under Edward III were frozen to death.

P. 50 L. 7   *wry-neck'd fife:* so called because the player turns his head sideways.

P. 50 L. 22   *Hagar's offspring:* Ishmaelites.

P. 50 L. 31   *Fast bind, fast find:* i.e., that which is bound fast will still be there when you come to look for it.

P. 51 L. 21   *scarfed:* i.e., gaily dressed with bunting on setting out for a voyage.

P. 53 L. 21   *draw aside the curtains:* In this Act Shakespeare uses all the devices of the Elizabethan stage. In the previous scene Jessica has first appeared on the balcony 'above'. Now the inner stage is used conveniently for the caskets, which are already in position to be discovered by drawing the curtain. See illustration, p. 13.

As o'er a brook: as if it were no more trouble than P. 55 L. 3
crossing a brook.

rib her cerecloth: to enclose her shroud (i.e., body). P. 55 L. 7
The cerecloth was the waxen covering in which the
bodies of the illustrious dead were wrapped.

coin ... angel: it was worth 10s. P. 55 L. 12

death: i.e., a skull. P. 55 L. 19

tombs: the texts read 'timber'. P. 55 L. 26

suit is cold: a proverb, 'you have lost your labour'. P. 55 L. 30

force and road of casualty: where misfortune comes P. 59 L. 2
most frequently.

cover: to put on the hat in the presence of an inferior. P. 59 L. 16

low peasantry ... honour: many low-born knaves P. 59
would be separated from true gentlefolk. LL. 18–19

sensible regreets: greetings full of feeling. P. 60 L. 32

costly: richly dressed. P. 61 L. 4

Bassanio Lord: This line is usually re-punctuated – P. 61 L. 11
'Bassanio, Lord Love, if thy will it be.' Actually
Nerissa is praying that Bassanio may be the new Lord
of Belmont.

slips of prolixity: slipping into excessive talk. P. 61 L. 25

full stop: i.e., cease this roundabout talk and come to P. 61 L. 29
the point.

here in Genoa: This is the reading of the texts; which P. 64 L. 16
perhaps should be 'heard in Genoa?' Some editors
emend to 'Where? in Genoa?'

treason there ... love: because the rack was used to P. 66 L. 5
extort confession from those accused of treason.

swan-like end: it was believed that swans, just before P. 66 L. 23
death, broke into song for the first and only time.

Alcides ... virgin tribute ... Dardanian wives: Alcides P. 67 LL. 1–4
(Hercules) rescued Hesione, daughter of Laomedon,
King of Troy, from the monster sent by Poseidon
(Neptune).

Here music ... caskets: As various commentators P. 67
have pointed out, Portia is hardly playing fair. With LL. 9–10
Bassanio saying to himself 'Gold? Silver? Lead?', the

rhymes 'fancy *bred*', 'in the *head*' are at least strongly suggestive.

P. 67 L. 29 *no vice:* the modern texts read 'voice'.

P. 68 L. 2 *valour's excrement:* a soldier's beard.

P. 68 LL. 3–6 *beauty . . . purchas'd . . . lightest:* i.e., beauty is too often bought and artificial, and those who most buy it are the lightest (or in modern phrase 'fast').

P. 68 LL. 7–11 *crisped . . . sepulchre:* 'So too those curly locks which wave in the wind are not genuine, but belonged to another, and often to a corpse' – for the wigmaker was not over-particular whence he obtained his hair.

P. 68 L. 14 *Indian beauty:* dark beauty. At this time fair skin was alone considered beautiful, as Shakespeare brutally pointed out in the Sonnets to the Dark Lady.

P. 68 L. 17 *Hard food for Midas:* Midas having been granted the fulfilment of anything he might wish, asked that whatever he touched should be turned to gold – which was embarrassing at meal times.

P. 68 L. 18 *pale . . . drudge:* silver, because used for common trade.

P. 69 L. 23 *by note:* as instructed.

P. 71 L. 15 *beheld the maid:* There was nothing incongruous in Gratiano's falling in love with Portia's maid for the personal attendants on noblemen and their wives were of gentle birth.

P. 71 L. 16 *for intermission:* to fill in the time.

P. 72 L. 8 *Youth . . . here:* i.e., if one so new to this place which is now mine.

P. 73 L. 1 *shrewd contents:* bitter news.

P. 73 LL. 13–14 *all . . . veins:* i.e., except for gentle birth I have nothing.

P. 78 L. 22 *to Padua:* the old texts read Mantua, but this is obviously a mistake for Padua.

P. 78 L. 25 *imagin'd speed:* quick as thought.

P. 78 L. 26 *Tranect:* the word is not used elsewhere; probably it means ferry.

P. 81 L. 7 *the Moor:* This is obviously a topical reference to some lady of the suburbs otherwise unknown to fame.

P. 81 L. 18 *cover:* lay the table; but Launcelot also puns on *cover*: put on my hat, which would be unmannerly of the servant before his master.

humours and conceits: whims and fancies. P. 81 L. 28

words are suited: forced to suit his purpose. P. 81 L. 30

The original reading of the text is here kept. Some- P. 84 L. 16 thing seems to have gone wrong. Modern editors often read 'urine; for affection, master of passion, sways it, etc.'

woollen bag-pipe: bag-pipe in a woollen covering. P. 84 L. 22

In the Quarto some words have been omitted from P. 85 L. 7 the beginning of these lines which read 'height,/ well use question with the Woolfe,/ the Ewe bleake for the Lambe.' The Folio corrects to 'Or even as well use question with the Wolfe,/ The Ewe bleate for the Lambe.' The lines are printed as usually emended by editors.

Pythagoras: a Greek philosopher and scientist whose P. 87 L. 3 teachings had great influence on European thought. Amongst other doctrines he taught the transmigration of souls.

Govern'd a Wolf: This is probably a reference to Dr P. 87 L. 6 Lopez, who was sometimes called Lopus (*lupus*: a wolf). See Introduction, p. 17.

A Daniel come to judgement: The remark refers to the P. 89 L. 31 story of Daniel told in *The History of Susanna* in the Apocrypha. Susanna was falsely accused of adultery by two Elders and was being led away to execution when 'the Lord raised up the holy spirit of a young youth, whose name was Daniel'. Daniel caused the two Elders to be examined separately when their testimony was shown to be false.

Barrabas: Shylock presumably refers to Barabbas P. 92 L. 10 'who for a certain sedition made in the city, and for murder, was cast into prison' whom Pilate released instead of Jesus (Luke 23 : 18–19); unless he is referring to Marlowe's Barrabas, the Jew of Malta, also an undesirable son-in-law.

two godfathers . . . ten more: i.e., twelve jurymen to P. 95 find you guilty. LL. 19–20

Know . . . again: a polite phrase – 'I hope we shall P. 96 L. 9

become better acquainted' – but used ironically.

P. 97 L. 26   *upon more advice:* on further consideration.

P. 98 L. 6   *old swearing:* 'any amount of swearing'.

P. 98 L. 31   *old Aeson:* Jason's father whom Medea by magic restored to youth again.

P. 99   *she doth stray about . . . holy hermit:* Dr Johnson observed: 'I do not perceive the use of this hermit, of whom nothing is seen or heard afterwards. The Poet had first planned his fable some other way, and inadvertently, when he changed his scheme, retained something of the original design.' Actually there is no difficulty. Portia (P. 77, L. 28 – P. 78, L. 4) has already explained her absence from Belmont to Lorenzo by saying that she and Nerissa intend to visit a monastery. The messenger's words are simply a confirmation of this fiction.
LL. 21–25

P. 99 L. 32   *Sola, sola:* Launcelot imitates the note of the postboy who announced his arrival by blowing his horn.

P. 100 L. 1   *Sola, did you see . . . :* The old texts read 'Sola, did you see M. *Lorenzo* and M. *Lorenzo* sola, sola.'

P. 100   *orb . . . sings:* Pythagoras taught that each of the planets in their passage through the heavens emitted a musical note, all together producing a heavenly harmony.
LL. 23–4

P. 100 L. 27   *muddy vesture of decay:* the mortal body which prevents the soul from hearing the heavenly harmony.

P. 100 L. 29   *Diana:* She was also the Moon.

P. 101 L. 32   *Nothing . . . respect:* Or as Hamlet put it, 'There's nothing good or bad but thinking makes it so'.

P. 103   *We . . . sun:* if you chose always to walk in the dark it would be light with us at the same time as on the opposite side of the globe; i.e., your presence makes darkness light.
LL. 1–2

P. 103 L. 16   *scant . . . courtesy:* cut short a welcome of mere words.

P. 103 L. 23   *posy:* inscription engraved on the inside of a ring.

P. 105 L. 21   *civil Doctor:* Doctor of Civil Law.

P. 106 L. 8   *Argos:* the all-seeing, because he had a hundred eyes.

P. 108 L. 17   *intergatories:* interrogatories, a list of questions on oath put to a witness or a suspected person.

GLOSSARY

accomplish'd: equipped
achieved: won
address'd: prepared
advised: careful
affection: natural disposition
agitation: for cogitation
ague: fever
alablaster: alabaster
Alcides: Hercules
allay: moderate
appropriation: special excellence
argosy: large merchant ship
aspect: countenance
attended: noted

bankrout: bankrupt
bate: lessen
beshrew: ill luck to
blood: desire
bootless: vain
bottom: ship
break: go bankrupt
break up: open a letter

cater-cousins: good friends
ceremony: holy object
commodity: advantage
complexion: natural instinct
compromis'd: agreed
conceit: (1) thought; (2) apprehension

confess: acknowledge
constant: well-balanced
continent: that which contains
contrive: plot
converted: transferred
cope: encounter
crisped: curly
cross: thwart

Dardanian: Trojan
death: skull
deface: cancel
deliberate: calculate
determine: decide
difference: dispute
discover: reveal
doit: small Dutch coin, half a farthing

eanlings: newborn lambs
ecstasy: madness, excitement
egal: equal
election: choice
engaged: run into debt
envious: hateful
equal: exact
Erebus: Hell
estimation: worth
excess: interest
expect: await

fall: mischance

fancy: love
fashion: manner
fear'd: made to fear
fearful: to be feared
fill-horse: cart-horse
flat: sandbank
flourish: ceremonial trumpet call
fond: foolish
fore-spurrer: fore-runner
forsworn: perjured
fulsom: fat

gaberdine: cloak
gag'd: pledged
garnish: ornament
gear: matter
gentle: with a pun on Gentile
gondilo: gondola
gratify: reward
gree: agree
gross: full sum
guarded: ornamented with braid
guiled: deceitful

habit: guise
highday: holiday, gay
humility: kindness
humour: whim

impeach: accuse
intermission: pastime

knapp'd: chewed

likely: handsome
lodg'd: firm fixed
lottery: lucky draw

martlet: martin
mere: absolute
misconster'd: misconstrued
mo: more
moiety: part

narrow seas: the English Channel
naughty: worthless
neat: ox

o'er-look'd: bewitched
offend'st: harmest
opinion: reputation
ostent: outward appearance
overname: repeat

pack: run away
passion: emotion
parts: actions
patch: fool
patens: small plates
pawn'd: pledged
peize: weigh down
penthouse: projecting eaves
plots: plans
port: standing
possessed: informed
posy: inscription inside a ring
preferr'd: promoted
presently: immediately
prest: ready

prevented: forestalled

purse: put into bags

quaintly: neatly

qualify: allay, moderate

quality: manner

rack'd: stretched

reason'd: conversed

reasons: intelligent remarks

reddest: bravest

reed voice: fluty voice

remorse: pity

reproach: for approach

rhenish: white Rhine wine

ripe: mature, needing attention

roads: safe anchorages

sad: serious

scant: make less

scanted: limited

school: university

scrubbed: scrubby

scruple: lit., 20 grains

season'd: garnished

sentences: wise sayings

shaft: arrow

shrive: give absolution

skipping: lively, frivolous

slubber: finish off hastily

sonties: little saints

Sophy: Shah

sort: dispose

sped: done for

spet: spit

stayed: waited

stead: help

still: continually, always

strond: strand, shore

surfeit: suffer from excess

tenour: intention of a legal agreement

thrift: profit

tucket: trumpet call announcing an arrival

turkis: turquoise

uncheck'd: not denied

unthrift: thriftless

untread: retrace

usance: interest, usury

vailing: lowering

varnish'd: painted, i.e., masked

via: go off

virgin hue: i.e., white

void: eject

waft: waved to

wis: I wis, assuredly

wroth: ruth, ruin

younger: gay young man

PENGUIN POPULAR CLASSICS

PENGUIN POPULAR CLASSICS

Published or forthcoming

PENGUIN POPULAR CLASSICS

PENGUIN POPULAR CLASSICS

PENGUIN POPULAR CLASSICS

PENGUIN POPULAR POETRY

Published or forthcoming

The Selected Poems *of:*

Matthew Arnold
William Blake
Robert Browning
Robert Burns
Lord Byron
John Donne
Thomas Hardy
John Keats
Rudyard Kipling
Alexander Pope
Alfred Tennyson
William Wordsworth
William Yeats

and collections of:

Seventeenth-Century Poetry
Eighteenth-Century Poetry
Poetry of the Romantics
Victorian Poetry
Twentieth-Century Poetry
Scottish Folk and Fairy Tales